Only the Truth

ALSO BY PAT BROWN

The Profiler
Killing for Sport
How to Save Your Daughter's Life (Sept 2012)
The Murder of Cleopatra (2013)

Only the Truth

Pat Brown

Published by Pat Brown, 2012.

ONLY THE TRUTH

First edition. March 12, 2012.

ISBN: 979-8227729026

Written by Pat Brown.

Only the Truth

PAT BROWN

For
all those
brave souls
who seek
the truth

Only
the
Truth

I

She was just standing there by the side of the railroad tracks, not seeming to know where she was. There hadn't been any trains in hours, nor would there be for the rest of the day. She was standing there like a statue, with the little red suitcase beside her.

She wasn't real pretty, but she was hardly ugly. She was a tiny thing with light brown hair that hung limply onto her shoulders. She made me think of my dog, which maybe isn't too nice a thing to say about a girl, but her hair reminded me of my dog's fur, soft and long, but also worn and tired.

"Hey, girl!" I yelled at her as I came up the bank onto the gravel. "Whatcha doing there?" I wasn't worried too much about scaring her. I never seemed to cause much fright to anyone. I was too short and too skinny. I didn't look like I'd harm nobody.

She gave me a slight smile, but she didn't answer. She just looked my way. I came right up in front of her, waiting for her to speak, but she didn't. She had clear, sky blue eyes that looked kind of empty, but I found myself staring in them, searching them for something, anything.

Then, I reached out and touched her shoulder.

She didn't flinch. She didn't move a muscle. She didn't even seem to feel my hand there. She just kept looking at me. It was a strange feeling, staring into someone's eyes, eyes that never blinked and just kept staring back at you. I wondered if she was reading my mind and whether she would be able to know more about what I was thinking than I did. Hell, I didn't even know what I was thinking.

She finally spoke. "Who are you?"

"Billy Ray."

She seemed to think about my name a bit. Then she said, "Can I go with you, Billy Ray?"

She said it so plain and sweet, I didn't know what she meant.

"Go with me?" She looked lost but I didn't understand what she wanted.

She kept her eyes locked on mine, still not blinking. "Just with you?"

I didn't have no one at home. No momma. No daddy. No family. Just the one dog. She didn't seem like she would be a problem to me, so I picked up her bag and took her hand and we walked out of town and the three miles up Makin Road to my place.

****

There is no real understanding Charlene. But then I never learned much of anything about women, so I didn't think I had to make work of it. Besides, Charlene don't ever get mad at me. She cooks like the Mama I never had and maybe if she had shown up twenty years ago when I was still a growin' boy she would have made a real man out of me. Now, all them biscuits she puts out make me round in the middle, but I ain't complainin' and she laughs and pats me there, so she ain't complainin' neither.

My dog likes her and that's saying a lot. He knows good when he comes into good. Charlene likes him, too. She feeds him her food before she even starts into her own, and she lets him keep his place on the bed beside me with no complainin' about no dirty dog gonna be sleepin' in her bed.

I ain't never had been with a girl before and she says she's never had no one before neither, and when we lie down for the first time, I'm scared and she's scared and I don't know what to do to make her happy. I never hung with the boys and I never went to look at dirty movies so I don't know what girls like, but then Charlene says I'm doing all right and I keep doing what she says is all right till she smiles and whispers my name like I never heard no one say my name before.

And she adds "Sweet" before it, saying "Sweet Billy Ray, Sweet Billy Ray." She says she likes running her hand through my hair, with its tight curly and steel-pad feel. She likes to rub her face over my hair, too, but if I get stubble on my chin, she makes me go straight to the shaving kit and make it smooth again.

I don't know why she likes it so rough on the top of my head but not on my face.

So I don't let her shave her legs like she wants. Her hair there is soft and I like running my hand over it. Sometimes we jest like curlin' up on the bed, forgettin' to get up and do anything, feelin' each other all over until we get so hungry I make Charlene cook something for me. I never had much good in my life before Charlene came, just days of sweeping up the streets in town and heatin' up the frozen food I buy at the Acme and sittin' on the porch with Big Dog.

Somethin' was always missing from my life but I didn't know it was missing until Charlene came along. Now I finally have someone to talk to besides myself and someone to listen to my stories, and she likes my stories and she asks me to tell 'em to her again and again even though she already knows exactly how they all end.

****

Charlene won't never leave the house. She won't go to town and do shopping like you would expect girls to do. She never asks about what I do in town when I come home from my work, and even if I tell her about 'bout something happened, she never asks no questions and after a while I just don't even talk about anythin' outside our four walls.

She's strange, but she's nice, so I let her be whatever way she wants to be. One day, she hung some garlic cloves right inside the front door and when I asked her what she did that for, she told me it was to keep the vampires out. I laughed cause I never heard of no vampires in these parts; lots of ghosts and spirits, but no vampires.

I thought she was being silly. I should have paid attention to her and left that garlic hanging there. It was the first of the mistakes I made that started all the trouble with Charlene.

****

He moved in across the road about a month before our second anniversary. That old house across the way had been empty for as long as I remember. Don't know who owned it and never thought of anyone living there. I was the only one who ever lived on this road since my aunty died when I was fourteen and then I jest kept livin' in the house alone till Charlene came if you don't count Big Dog who showed up when I was about twenty.

****

He was an old guy. He was white like Charlene, but his skin wasn't creamy like hers. Must be he spent his life in the fields and that made him look two shades darker. His hair was long and gnarled up like he didn't know 'bout brushin' it. He had a mustache and a beard that covered most of his face and since his hair hung down long over it, best you could see was just his eyes. I wandered over cross the road and looked at him more closely and he smelt of liquor.

He nodded and grunted; I guessed it was a hello. Then he walked away and went back around the side of his house. I went back to my side of the road and the first week he lived there, the old man across the road stayed to himself and never set foot outside. I never went back over to his side of the road, and he never came over to ours.

****

Charlene sat with me on the back porch with our lemonades. It was a hot June day and we could hear Big Dog across the street, barking.

"What's he barking at?" Charlene asked me. "I've been listening to him bark all week long and I never heard him bark 'cept for when you come back from town at night."

I told her about the old man who'd moved in. I told her he was her color and he stunk of liquor and he didn't seem too interested in talkin' much. Charlene and I took to sittin' on the back porch in the evening, listenin' to Big Dog cause a ruckus every time that man must have opened his front door. Didn't bother us none; it would have all been fine if the old man had just stayed over on his side of the road.

****

The old man suddenly decided to be neighborly; at least that's what I was guessin' when he showed up at the front door. Charlene was in the back bedroom and I guess she didn't hear the knock or she might have told me to tell whoever was knocking to go the hell away. But she wasn't there to tell me and so I opened the door.

Even worse, I pulled down the garlic that hung in the doorway lest it scare our visitor away. When I opened the door he didn't say nothing, just stood there, so I told him to come on in though I didn't know what I was inviting him in for.

Charlene must have heard the door open or me talkin' and she came out of the bedroom. She took a few steps into the room and when she saw the old man at the door, she just stood still and didn't offer any greeting. The old man muttered something about sugar, and seein' that Charlene wasn't movin' toward the kitchen, I went over and scooped two cupfuls into a paper bag and brought it to the old man. It took me a minute to get his attention to take the sack because he was looking at Charlene in a way I damn well didn't like.

I wanted him to go then, and I shoved the paper sack at him and stood between him and Charlene, and he grabbed it out of my hand, turned and left. I never saw him again.

Charlene stopped talkin' three days later. She stopped askin' to hear my stories. She moved through the day like the hours was pressin' heavy against her. She didn't leave the house to sit on the back porch with me and she took to using a chamber pot rather than the outhouse. She still did the cookin' and the washin', but I began to feel like I was alone in the house with just Big Dog again.

I figured it was just some temporary thing, that Charlene would come around in a day or so, but nothing changed all that week, or the next week, or the next.

****

My other mistake was going out for cigarettes on our second anniversary. Charlene made a nice dinner and afterwards I presented her with a Hostess cupcake with a candle in it. She almost smiled and that made me smile and I helped her blow out the candle and I danced around the room with her and it seemed like she was the old Charlene again. I felt like maybe we was going to be happy like we used to be. I should have kept on dancing with her but I wanted some cigarettes cause I had run out, and I wanted to buy Charlene some candy. But to be honest, I probably wouldn't have gone out to get Charlene candy if I hadn't really been craving a cigarette, so it was thinking about me, not her, that let the bad thing happen.

"I'll be back in a jiffy," I told her and jumped behind the wheel of my truck. I'd just got her for $100 off of Melvin, who owned the liquor store in town, and said his new truck was too sweet to be parked next to that "Piece of Crap" on wheels, his dented Ford pick-up that was almost as old as he was. Piece of Crap may be headed for the junkyard soon, but for now, it was good for someone like me who just needed a ride once in a while if there was somethin' like an emergency. We got no phone to be callin' for

an ambulance so if Charlene would get sick or hurt, I needed some way to get to the big city. Piece of Crap was all banged up and made lots of noises I didn't know nothing about, but Mel told me I could pay him $10 a week till I owned the whole truck and if it broke down before I got to the ten-week final payment, then he would give me my money back.

I really never drove much before, but there ain't no traffic on the dirt road between my house and the town, so I can't kill nobody if I drive bad.

I walked into Tom's Grocery to get me the cigarettes and candy. "I need me some of that candy you got there for my girlfriend," I said, pointing to the jar near the cash register. "And I need me some smokes." I realized for the first time since Charlene showed up, I had said something about her to someone else. I guess I'd always been afraid saying she was with me might jinx her staying.

Lizzie raised her eyebrow and looked surprised as all get out, handed me over my cigarettes and a handful of the little drops in the jar. I grinned and walked back to my truck, feeling like a grown man for the first time in my thirty-four years of life.

I must have smiled all the way home cause my jaws was achin' when I turned up the mountain. Then I saw the smoke. There was a glow up toward the house and it already felt hotter as I drove up the hill. I knew I was panicking cause I was breathing way too fast. I pressed my foot to the floor but the truck didn't seem to know how to go any faster and it took what seemed like an hour to climb that steep hill.

I couldn't see over the top of it so I didn't know if the whole forest was on fire. Finally, Piece of Crap bumped over the last rise in the road and I could see a house on fire. Took me a moment for the relief to wash over me that it wasn't mine. It was the old man's house across the way. The thing was blazin' pretty darn good and I could hardly make out the structure, but lucky no wind was blowing and the little house just looked like a well-kept fire someone was watchin' as they burnt up a bunch of scrap wood and old furniture. As I pulled up, I could make out the stove and a couch through the flames, but I didn't see the old man in there.

I thought maybe he had gone to town when the place went up but then I hadn't see him on the road either way so I figured he should be somewhere around. He wasn't the type to sleep during the day, so the fire couldn't have caught him unawares. From my porch, I could always see him movin' around, nervous as a cat, probably stinking of drink, but the drink never seemed to put him down. I wasn't even sure the man slept at night.

As I pulled up to our house, I didn't see him outside and Charlene wasn't outside neither. I jumped out of the truck and raced into the house. "Charlene! Where are you, Charlene?"

"I'm right here," she said and she was. She was sitting just inside the front door looking out the window and she looked happy. She had a slight smile on her face and it was then that I realized she had spoken for the first time in a month.

"Is the old man in there?" I asked her.

"He's in there," she answered. She smiled bigger this time.

"Did you try to get him out?"

"No."

I stopped asking her questions and together we watched the house burn itself to the ground. Our house was ungodly hot from the summer heat and what with the fire burning so close, we sat there with sweat pouring down our faces. But we sat there anyway, mesmerized by the fire. I was just happy to be with Charlene, a Charlene with a smile on her face who was talking again. Charlene who just seemed to be happy watching her neighbor's house burn down. And if she was happy, so was I.

****

Sheriff Hathaway showed up in time to watch the last bit of the flames sputter out. I joined him on the road.

"What the hell happened?" he asked, wiping his eyes with a hanky to get the ash out of them.

I shook my head. "I dunno. When I left for town, the house was there. When I came back, it was near gone."

The Sheriff squinted through the smoke over at the remains of the house." Do you know anything about the old man who moved in there? When I first run up on him in town, he told me his name was Otis Barnes, and since no one ever had a complaint about him, I never asked much more about him. He bought his groceries and liquor once a week. That was it. I passed him a few times on the road." The Sheriff shook his head. "I got no clue where he come from or what he was doing here. No one seems to know."

I couldn't tell him nothing more. "Never talked to me. Kept to his side of the road." I didn't tell him how his moving in seemed to have made Charlene go silent.

The Sheriff nodded toward the house. "I hear you got yourself a girl?"

I grinned. "Yep."

"Who's the girl?"

I told him her name. "Charlene."

"What's her last name?"

Took me a while to think about that question. I could feel the Sheriff's eyes on me but I didn't have no answer to tell him. She'd never told me her last name and I guess I never asked it.

I looked at my feet. "Don't know."

I heard the Sheriff sigh.

"Where'd she come from?"

"Don't know."

The Sheriff look exasperated.

"Come on, Billy Ray. Take me on inside to meet this girl of yours." He opened the front door and I walked him into the house.

I pointed toward Charlene in the chair next to the window. "There she is. There's my Charlene."

The Sheriff took off his hat. "Ma'am." He nodded at her.

She nodded back. "Sir." At least Charlene was still speaking.

"You see what happened?"

Charlene nodded again, "There was a fire."

"Did you see how it started?"

"It just started." She still had that faraway look in her eye.

The Sheriff pursed his lips. He ran his hanky over his face and neck. He was perspiring a lot, as stifling as it was with that heat in the air.

"Did you see the old man leave the house?"

Charlene shook her head. "No."

"Do you know if the old man was in the house?" The Sheriff emphasized "was in the house."

"Yes."

"Yes, you know, or, yes, he was?"

"Yes." She stated again. "Yes, he was."

"Was he drunk?"

"Probably."

Sheriff Hathaway looked like he was becoming irritated.

"Did you try to save him?"

"No."

I pulled on the Sheriff's arm. "Come out on the porch, Sheriff. I need to talk to you." I didn't like the way he was looking at Charlene, not understanding her.

The air on the porch, although it was still hot from the fire, felt good compared to the air in the house.

The Sheriff wiped at his face again. His hanky was drenched so it likely didn't help much.

"What's wrong with that girl?" he asked.

"She's just Charlene. She's quiet like that. She don't talk much. She don't go out of the house. Even if she saw the fire, she wouldn't go out of the house. She just don't go out of the house."

The Sheriff sighed. "All right, Billy Ray. I won't ask her nothing more right now." He opened the door to his patrol car. "I'll be back up with those fire folks from the city. You two just keep staying on your side of the road so you don't mess up nothing."

I nodded. I couldn't see the point of walking around over there anyhow.

That night Charlene and I made love, and she whispered "Sweet Billy Ray" when she shuddered.

****

Life had returned to normal. Charlene was back to cooking and laughing, Charlene and I slept like spoons together on the bed with Big Dog. The Sheriff came with a bunch of other cars and men to the burned-up house across the road and for days I watched them sifting through the ashes from my front porch. Charlene never came out to watch, but she left out the back of the house to go to the latrine and I didn't have to clean the chamber pot any more.

Finally, the men went away, leaving the remains of the fire to be grown over by the woods. I could see little pine trees starting to pop up between the ashes and some clinging vines working their way up the burnt out stove and refrigerator. I started feeling my two mistakes were being forgotten.

Then Sheriff Hathaway came back. I saw him step out of his car and stand in front of the house looking none too happy. He had some other policeman with him. He turned to him and said something and then came to the front door. I opened it before he knocked.

He cleared his throat and said he was sorry he had to come.

Then he told me to step outside.

He put his hand on my shoulder. "We have to talk some more, Billy Ray."

"Okay." I didn't know what about.

"I'll come straight to the point." He took his hand off my shoulder. "That old man was killed."

I wasn't understanding what he was telling me this for. "Oh. Well, then you found him in the house." I figured as much, since no one saw him since the fire.

The Sheriff cleared his throat again. He took out his hanky and wiped his face, even though the day was cool. "No, Billy Ray, you aren't getting me. The old man was killed before the fire started. He was shot with his rifle."

"He killed hisself?"

"No, Billy Ray, he was shot. The ballistics people say he was shot above his ear from a ways away. Seems like he was sitting on the side of his bed when he was shot. He fell on the floor and that's where he was when the fire burnt him up."

I shook my head. "I didn't see no one come up the road before I left and I didn't see no one on the way back. Maybe someone came up while I was in the store."

The Sheriff shifted from one foot to the other. He mopped at his face again.

"Billy Ray, the old man was killed, then the fire was set with gasoline."

I didn't say nothing. I didn't really understand what the Sheriff was getting at.

"Billy Ray, where's your gas can? The one you had in your truck?"

I shrugged. "I'm guessing it's in the truck."

"Why don't we take a look, Billy Ray?" The Sheriff started over to my truck and I followed him. We looked in the bed and I didn't see anything.

"Where's the can, Billy Ray?"

"I dunno. It was there before."

"Before when?"

"Before...," I didn't know when before, except I had seen it before today, sometime before today.

I shook my head. "I dunno."

The Sheriff slumped back against the side of the truck. "We found the can, Billy Ray, out in the woods behind the old man's house."

"My can?"

"Well, it was a gas can."

Lots of people got gas cans in their trucks around these parts. The gas station wasn't open some days and it was easy to get stuck with no gas in the tank. I never bought more than a few dollars when the tank was empty cause I never needed much and I never had much to spend. But I kept that gas can full in case there was reason to need to get to the city on a day the tank might be empty. Same for other folks.

"How do you know it's my gas can, Sheriff? It wasn't no special can. Just one the station gave me."

The Sheriff looked at me very seriously." You understand anything about evidence testing, Billy Ray?"

"No."

"Well, Billy, they can do this testing these days on all kinds of things. They did some testing on that can. There was a dent in the can, Billy Ray, a dent with some paint in it. They tested that paint."

I still didn't understand what that would tell him. "Paint?"

"Paint. Orange paint. What color is your truck, Billy Ray?"

"Orange."

Sheriff Hathaway looked right at me. "Did that old man do something to your girl, Billy Ray? Something you didn't like?"

I was feeling scared now. I wondered why he was looking at me that way and asking me what the old man had done to Charlene. "I dunno. She started actin' strange after he come here that one day but I never knew that he done anythin' to her."

"Why did you go to town that evening?"

"I was out of cigarettes. I wanted to buy Charlene some candy."

"Are you sure you weren't looking for a reason not to be home when the fire started? You knew Charlene wouldn't leave the house, but wouldn't you have left the house to save the old man if you were there?"

I started to cry because now the Sheriff was saying I killed the old man.

He put his arm around me and pushed me toward the police car, nodding to the other officer, who opened the back door for me. The Sheriff slid his hand up to the top of my head and pushed down on it so I wouldn't hit myself on the doorframe.

The two of them got in the car and said nothing more. We drove to the station in town. I cried all the way because Charlene wouldn't know what happened to me and I didn't know what was happening to me.

****

"Roll your finger like this," the younger police officer said and showed me how to ink each finger and press it into the little box on the cardboard square. All my fingers and my thumbs turned black and then I was allowed to wash them with some special soap.

I spent the day in a cell with time out for sitting in a little room to talk with the Sheriff. He kept asking me the same questions about what the old man might have done to Charlene that made me so mad I would want to kill him. But all I wanted was to go home to Charlene.

"If I tell you, will you let me see Charlene?"

"Sure, Billy Ray."

"Okay." I tried to think hard. "He was a dirty old man and he was drunk all the time and he said dirty things about Charlene. I thought he would hurt her."

The Sheriff nodded. "So you decided she would be safer if he was gone?"

I looked at him and what he said seemed to make sense. "Yeah, she would be safer."

"So you went over to his house?"

"Yeah, I went over to his house."

"And you shot him with his gun?"

"Yeah, I shot him with his gun."

The Sheriff looked pleased. "Then you went and got your gas can out of the truck?"

"Yeah."

"And you got some matches from the kitchen?"

"Yeah."

"And you poured the gas around the house and lit a match?"
"Yeah."
"Then what did you do with the gas can and the matches?"
"I threw them behind the house in the woods?"
"Okay."

I was doing good now. I could see the Sheriff was happy. "Then I went to town."

The Sheriff had written all this down while I was talking. "Good job, Billy Ray. Now sign right here at the bottom that what you said was the truth."

I signed the paper where he pointed at. "Can I go see Charlene now?"
The Sheriff looked down at the paper. "Maybe later."

****

I was put back in the cell. He didn't let me see Charlene. I watched out the cell and I could see the Sheriff and the other policemen writing lots of papers and whispering among themselves. It got to be lunch time and they brought me a sandwich and a soda pop. I was just finishing my sandwich when the whispering stopped and I heard the Sheriff say, "What?" and another officer say, "No kidding." I could see everyone gathered around the Sheriff, who was staring at a piece of paper.

Then he ran his hand through his hair and walked back to the desk where I could still see the paper I had signed lying there on the corner. He picked it up, shook his head, and then crumbled the paper in his right hand. He threw it in the wastebasket by the desk. He cussed under his breath but I couldn't hear the swear word. Then he looked over at me and pulled the cell keys out of his pocket.

He unlocked the cell door and motioned for me to come out. "I'm taking you home, Billy Ray," he said wearily, not looking me in the eye.
"To see Charlene?" I asked.
"Yeah, you can see Charlene."
"Am I comin' back?"

The Sheriff didn't look at me. "No, Billy Ray. You won't be coming back. You're free." I wondered why he didn't think I killed the old man now.

****

I was nearly bursting when we topped the hill to the house. I was going to see my Charlene. When we pulled in front of the house, I was out of the police car nearly before it stopped, thanking them for the ride home. I rushed up to the front door and into the house and found Charlene standing at the window. I pulled her into my arms and hugged her tight and whispered that I hoped she hadn't worried about me. I kissed her and she smiled at me.

I heard a noise behind us and turned to find the Sheriff and the officer who drove me up here standing between us and the front door.

"Thanks, again, Sheriff," I told him. I wanted him to get on his way and leave me with my Charlene. But the Sheriff didn't move.

"Gotta talk to Charlene, Billy Ray."

I pulled away from Charlene and looked from her to him. "What for? I thought you said I was free."

The Sheriff moved closer and said, "You are, Billy Ray. I need to talk to Charlene a minute."

"Okay." He was confusing me again.

The Sheriff looked down at Charlene. He was a big man and she was no more than coming up to his shoulder.

"Charlene? Did you kill that old man?"

My stomach turned over. I felt myself breaking out into a cold sweat. Now he was going after Charlene. I didn't understand. I looked at Charlene's face, but she didn't look upset at the question.

"Charlene? Did you kill the old man?" The Sheriff asked the question over again.

Charlene didn't answer the question, but I saw her head move up and down.

The room suddenly seemed awfully hot. I felt dizzy.

I heard myself ask, "Why, Charlene? Why?"

Charlene just shrugged her shoulders.

My feet weren't steady under me and I found myself sittin' in the chair with the Sheriff holding my left arm. Then, I watched through the window as the Sheriff put Charlene into the police car, and all of a sudden I was alone again with Big Dog.

Charlene, who had never left the house in over two years, was gone.

II

I spent the night with Big Dog wrapped in my arms. I cried and Big Dog cried too, and we both whimpered through the night.

When morning came, I went out to start up the truck but the engine wouldn't turn over. The gas was all used up and when I got out to look in the back for my emergency fuel, I realized the can wasn't back there any more. A picture of Charlene pouring gas around the old man in the house flashed into my mind and I hit my head on the driver's door to make it stop. I could feel something wet start down my between my eyes and I tasted blood as the liquid came over my top lip.

I could hardly see through the blur in my eyes as I set off on foot into town. The three miles felt longer than they ever had before. I didn't know if it was because I had gotten used to driving the truck into town, or because I was walkin' slower and slower as I got towards Main Street.

I wanted to know the truth and I didn't want know the truth. I wanted my Charlene back and I wanted everyone to leave us alone.

When I got to the police station, I found the Sheriff. He winced and then he sat me down by his desk and I looked over at Charlene on the cot behind bars, sittin' just where I was the day before.

"Did she sign one of those papers you had me sign?" I asked him.

Sheriff Hathaway plucked at his collar, his face going red. I wasn't sure why he was so embarrassed, but he wouldn't look at me.

"She won't talk none, Billy Ray."

"Then how you gonna keep her here? If she didn't sign the paper, she can go home with me, can't she?"

"No, Billy Ray. We got proof she killed him. We got evidence."

I felt kind of sorry for the Sheriff. "Wasn't that the same evidence..." I pronounced the word "evidence" clear and careful, "that you said meant I killed the old man?"

The Sheriff shook his head and now he looked at me more firmly. "No, Billy Ray, we got real strong evidence now. We got a fingerprint on the box of matches that we found with the gas can; a box of matches just like the boxes in your kitchen, the ones you get from the Ben Franklin for lighting your stove."

"Whose fingerprint?"

"Hers, Billy Ray. Charlene's."

I actually laughed. "Well, she cooks in the kitchen. She lights the stove, don't she?" I was feeling pretty smart now.

The Sheriff became angry. "Her fingerprint, Billy Ray. On a brand new box of matches near the gas can from your truck. Only you or her could have killed that old man. Take your pick."

Only me or her.

I looked down at my hands in my lap. I made my fingers lock together and turn upside down. I heard a little song in my head that my Aunty sang to me when I was real little. "See all the people in the church"...or something like that.

I wished I could remember killing that old man. I really wished I could.

****

The second night without Charlene felt as bad as the first, but Big Dog whimpered a little less.

I went back to the Sheriff's office in the morning.

"You got my paper with my name on it saying what I did," I reminded him. "And I've been thinking all night about how you got my gas can and my matches from the kitchen. So since I said I did it, I must have did it."

The Sheriff just looked sadly at me. "Charlene said she did it, Billy Ray. She said she did it. You go ask her."

He pulled out the cell keys and let me into the cell. I sat down beside Charlene on the cot. We didn't touch, keeping our hands in our laps.

"Did you, Charlene? They say you did."

Charlene nodded yes, but she didn't say the words.

"Why, Charlene, why?" I remembered I already asked her that at the house.

She shrugged again.

I could feel myself getting angry. Not because she killed him, but because killing the man separated us and she didn't even seem to know why she done it. I grabbed her by the shoulders and turned her toward me. Then I grabbed her face in my hands and kissed her hard.

"Tell me why, Charlene? Tell me why?"

She cocked her head kind of funny to the side. I looked into her eyes and I felt like I was looking clear through her, like she was hardly there.

She stared back at me like she had done the first day we met and she said, "Who are you? Can I go home with you? Just go home?"

My hands dropped from the sides of her face and I called to the Sheriff, who'd been watchin' us, to let me out. I left without saying goodbye—to him, to her, to anyone between me and the road home.

****

I didn't go to work for the next two weeks. I couldn't stand seein' everybody in town, havin' them ask me questions about Charlene, about the trial. I couldn't stand lookin' at the Sheriff's office and thinkin' of Charlene in that jail cell. I couldn't stand that she never asked for me, like I didn't even exist for her anymore.

I felt like never goin' back to town. But then the food ran out and I had to get some money. When I was sweepin' the street, I looked straight down so when anyone came near I didn't have to talk to them and I kept my distance from the Sheriff's office.

At the end of the day, Mr. Millhouse gave me my money and I walked the three miles back home and crawled into bed with Big Dog. I finally slept through the night.

Life didn't change for the next two months. I went to work early and worked till after dark so I wouldn't have so much time awake at home to miss Charlene. Then a lawyer came and stirred up more pain and my nights of sound sleep were over.

****

He was a young boy. White, like Charlene. He knocked on my door on a Sunday morning and I was there because I didn't ever go to church and ever since Charlene was gone, I wasn't on very good terms with God either.

He looked apologetic, maybe because he was one of those righteous men they talk about, but then he wasn't at church neither, so he couldn't have been all that righteous. Plus he was a lawyer and I always heard one should keep as far away from lawyers as you should from doctors. They both brought bad news that you'd just as soon not hear.

"Can I come in?" he asked, looking all serious in his fancy shirt and tie. Made me wonder if he was on his way to church after all. No one ever came to my house in a tie...well, no one ever came to my house.

I waved him in and we sat in the two chairs by the front window. It was fall now and too cold to sit on the porch this early in the day.

"I'm Timothy Green," he stated, sticking his hand out. I shook it out of that courtesy stuff. I still had no idea who he was or what he was doing sitting in my house.

"I am Charlene's lawyer, "he explained. "I'm her court-appointed defense attorney."

I nodded. It hurt me to hear her name.

"She asked for you last week," he said.

I looked up. "She asked for me?"

"Well, she asked of you, I should say. She asked where that nice young man went to. She asked me every day."

I felt guilty. I should have gone to see her. Just because she killed a man and stopped knowing me....I swallowed hard.

The lawyer didn't look away when he saw me struggling with my conscience. "She really could use you to visit her. Maybe it will help her remember something. These things take time, you see. She has some kind of problem and I am trying to figure out what it is. I can't defend her without knowing who she is, where she came from, and what's going on in her mind."

He leaned forward, now very serious. "The prosecution has what they call an open-and-shut case. A 'slam dunk' it's called. They don't expect me to do anything but show up in court and say a few words about Charlene being a nice lady who made a mistake and then the jury will convict her and she will get a life sentence and we will all be home by lunch."

But I wasn't listening to the rest of it. All I could think was, Charlene wants to see me. She wants to see me.

****

I spent the whole day with Charlene in her jail cell. I brought her some sweets and she ate them and she smiled at me. She didn't say anything, but she let me talk to her and when I went to leave she hung onto me. She even let me kiss her and I felt her tongue warm in my mouth the way she used to do in bed. I only wish she had said my name.

I started visiting Charlene every day on my lunch break and before I went home in the evening. We was like a couple again excepting she didn't seem to know who I was and we couldn't lie in our bed together anymore. But I was there and she was there and so we was still together, in a way.

I began to worry about the trial. If Mr. Green was right, Charlene would go to court in a couple more months and then they would say she killed the old man and she would be taken away and we wouldn't be together for a long, long time. The real prison was hundreds of miles away and we would hardly get to see each other. My heart hurt when I thought about that but I didn't know how you stop people from saying she did it when the police said she did it and she herself said she did it. I finally told Mr. Green I would do anything to help Charlene keep out of prison and he came back up to the house so we could be away from prying eyes and ears.

Mr. Green took out a pad of paper from a shiny briefcase and pulled off the pen attached to it. He clicked it to its ready position and he asked me my name.

"Billy Ray Hutchins".

"Birthdate?"

"May 16, 1978".

"Where were you born?"

I guessed it was here. "Here in Whitfield Glen."

"Your momma or daddy alive?"

I shook my head. "Daddy died before I was born and Momma right after. My Aunty raised me here in this house."

A small smile played on Mr. Green's lips. "You ever go past town in your life, Billy Ray?"

I didn't quite know what was so funny about that. "No, I didn't have no call to."

"When did you meet Charlene?"

"Some two years ago."

"You and Charlene never got married, did you?"

"No." It never crossed my mind to do that and Charlene didn't ask me to go with her to no church or into any town office to sign no papers. It didn't seem like it was very important to get people's permission to love each other.

Mr. Green flipped the page he had been scribbling on over and started in on a fresh new one.

"Now, about Charlene. Do you know her full name?"

"I just know Charlene. That's what she told me."

"Do you know where she was born?"

"I thought here in Arkansas. She never talked 'bout no other state."

"How old is she?"

"She told me she was twenty-four the day we met."

"Did she talk about her family?"

"No. She never talked about no family. I figgered she didn't have one neither to talk about."

Mr. Green looked at me in an odd way.

"Did she ever talk about her children?"

I looked up sharply at Mr. Green to see if he was trying to make me say things that didn't make sense like Sheriff Hathaway did when he made me tell stories about killing that old man. "What children?"

Mr. Green looked at me quietly and spoke slowly. "She's had children, Billy Ray. Didn't she tell you about them?"

I shook my head back and forth and back and forth again. "She ain't had no children. She told me she had never been in love and never had no boyfriend. I was her first man. I could tell by the way she was so scared it would hurt and how embarrassed she was."

Mr. Green didn't speak. I knew I had him. "You making that up, aren't you, Mr. Green? She didn't say nothing about no children."

The lawyer licked his lips. He seemed awfully nervous. I don't know why he would tell me lies when we were supposed to be on the same side.

"No, Billy Ray, she didn't tell me about any children. She said she'd never had any children."

It felt good proving Mr. Green wrong about her having babies.

The lawyer went on. "Charlene didn't tell me she had any babies, but the doctor who examined her says she is a multipara."

I screwed up my face. "A what?"

"A multipara. That is the word for a woman who has had more than one child in her life."

I felt queasy.

"You okay, Billy Ray?"

"She was a virgin," I muttered. I couldn't even raise my eyes to look at Mr. Green again and when I heard the front door close I knew he had left me with my thoughts, to spend the night staring at the ceiling above the bed where Charlene had cried out when I entered her for the first time.

****

When I didn't show up at work the next morning, Mr. Green showed up on my doorstep. "I was waiting for you in town but ......" he smiled half apologetically.

I didn't feel like letting him in but I knew he wouldn't go away until I did.

He handed me a paper.

I turned it over and saw a bunch of typing. "I don't read good," I said and I handed it back to him. "Just tell me what it says."

"I'll give you the important details. It's the medical report the prosecution asked for. It says Charlene is a multipara..." I winced. He went on. "Well, what we discussed yesterday. The report also states she has had STDs before."

"STDs?"

"Sexually Transmitted Diseases. It means she got diseases from having sex with men. Have you ever had any STD's?" The lawyer wanted to know if I gave her any sickness.

"I never had no sex with any girl but Charlene." I hung my head. I had been teased about that by men in the liquor store. Some even offered to give me their sister for some money but I knew they were just playing with me and I never gave them my money.

The lawyer looked sad for me. I didn't know if it was that I never got none except from Charlene or that Charlene had gotten some somewhere else and never told me.

"Charlene has a history of STD's, Billy Ray. This means she got sick more than once from probably more than one man. We got some men from

about an hour away from here who say they know her from the street. Do you know what that means, Billy Ray?"

I knew what that meant. I had seen girls like that in town once in a while, passing through.

"Charlene didn't act like one of those girls. She wasn't one of those girls."

Mr. Green patted me on the shoulder and left me to spend another long day and night staring at the ceiling wondering what Charlene told the other men she lied under while she looked up at the stars, and the hotel plaster, and the little holes in the Ford vinyl roof liner. I cried so much I couldn't breathe after a while and I woke up Big Dog with my coughing and the two of us didn't get back to sleep the rest of the night.

****

I couldn't stand to go visit Charlene at the jail anymore. It wasn't just that she killed a man and that she didn't know who I was no more and it wasn't just that she lied to me about me being her first man and it wasn't about her being a whore. It was just I was scared I would hit her and I didn't want her to hate me for hitting her.

Mr. Green showed up and tried to convince me to go see her. I held the door open just a few inches and I kept my foot on the backside of it. I wasn't going to let him in the house to tell me anything more bad about Charlene.

He told me she was crying for me.

"She don't even know who I am," I countered.

"But she needs you to visit her anyway," he argued.

I didn't respond.

"I need you to visit her," he pleaded.

"What for? She don't tell me nothing."

"She might."

I laughed bitterly. "Well, she never slipped up all the time we spent here before she went to jail. All them hours we spent alone, everyday, just the two of us, talking and talking, and she never told me nothing about herself."

I slammed the door. I didn't want to start crying again. I wanted my Charlene back, the one I knew, the one I thought I knew. Even the one in jail was still my Charlene, but every time that lawyer talked to me, he made Charlene say and do horrible things. And when I went to sleep at night, Charlene would come into my dreams, getting nastier and nastier, cussing and screwing and birthing ugly babies. Then, I became afraid to go to the jail, not because I would hit her but because I was afraid she would act like the girl that visited me at night and I wouldn't be able to love her any more.

****

I went back to cleaning my streets, looking at the ground, and keeping away from jail cells, policemen, and lawyers. I swept and swept and this made up my days for the next few weeks and I pretended that the two of us were all that lived in the world...just me and Big Dog.

Of course, I wasn't deaf and I heard what they were saying about Charlene. Charlene or Jasmine or Sugar or whatever other name they say the men over in Bald Eagle knew her as. The prosecution wasn't being quiet about what they were going to say about Charlene in court. They were calling her a whore. A whore who used men and when she robbed a few men too many, she slipped out of town to hide from the police. She went up the mountain to Whitfield Glen and went home with the first sucker who would have her and ask no questions. That would be me.

They said bad things about me, too. They called me a retard and a weirdo. Said I never had much sense and it was only because I didn't cause no trouble and kept the town clean that they left me alone to myself up on the hill. They said I didn't bother no one so they didn't bother me.

They said no woman had ever gotten near me on account I was ugly looking and short and walked funny. They said if Charlene had been a prettier girl and not a whore, she wouldn't have let me touch her. I didn't trust no one no more.

The prosecution just added Charlene's motive for killing the old man cross the road. Seems that he was one of the men Charlene slept with for money, but that Charlene had stolen all the rest of the money he had. He was pissed off enough to want his money back and that's why he came out to the Glen. They said that while I was working she must have been crossing the road to sleep with him, to pay him back for what money of his she didn't have any more and to keep him quiet, so he wouldn't tell me what she was. Then they say she got tired of dealing with him and killed him so she would be free of him. Didn't make no sense to the that the old man would come all the way here and hang out across the road unless Charlene took him for a whole bunch of money and she didn't have none that I knew of when she came. But I hear that all a lawyer has to do is make up some story about why a person killed someone and if the jury was stupid enough to believe it, then it didn't matter if it was true or not.

And, in a way, it was a good story for me even if it seemed kind of dumb. I liked the idea she killed the old man because she loved me and didn't want me to know what kind of girl she had been before. She lied because she loved me and she killed because she loved me. She was my beautiful Charlene again. I started visiting her in the jail most days. She was happy to see me and she called me by my name though she still didn't seem to know who I was. They let me see her every evening for as long as I wanted and I started to pretend the cell was our little home. The guard on duty in the evening went out for a long smoke between eight and nine o'clock and let us make love on the little cot.

The defense asked for another month's delay which the judge granted and Charlene and I spent the autumn happy in our new home, eating our dinner together, and making love as soon as the policeman winked, pulled out his cigarette pack and stepped out the front door. Charlene didn't seem so much different than when we were in our house. We were Charlene and Billy Ray again and I started growing fearful of the trial that would proclaim her guilty of her love crime and take her away again.

****

It was during our Thanksgiving TV dinner in the cell that I heard the defense lawyer got the trial postponed again until the New Year. I whooped and hollered and kissed Charlene a dozen times on the lips! She smiled just a little at me.

"Don't you know what this means, Charlene?" I said, squeezing her close to me.

She shook her head.

"We got another two months together before we got to worry about anything! We're gonna have our third Christmas together!"

Charlene smiled at how happy I was. She kissed me and wanted to make love right away but the guard wasn't ready to go out for his cigarette just yet. She didn't seem to understand anything about her trial. She never got upset or scared or angry. She didn't seem to worry about anything now. She just saw me happy and it made her happy. When she is happy, she likes to make love and so I like to make her happy.

I leaned over to kiss her again and she put her finger to my lips and then she went over to the cell bars and called to the guard. He came over and she crooked her finger at him. He leaned his ear over to the bars and she whispered something in it that made him grin. Then he shot a thumbs up at me, grabbed his cigarettes and left the room, an hour before the appointed time. We made love over and over that evening and he didn't come back until midnight.

****

I was still in bed the next day recovering from my night with Charlene when I heard the screech of tires by the side of the house. I slid out of bed, told Big Dog to shut up and reached the front door just as the banging started. It was Mr. Green, looking real angry. I didn't have to guess he was bringing more bad lawyer news and this time somehow the bad news had to do with me.

"I need you to be honest with me, Billy Ray." I noticed Mr. Green wasn't wearing a tie this time when he came visiting.

I wondered what I had done wrong.

"Have you been screwing Charlene in the jail cell?"

I wondered why Mr. Green cared. Lovemaking was between a girl and a guy. What did he want to know for?

"Why are you asking? She's my girl, ain't she?" I said defensively.

Mr. Green pulled off his coat and tossed it on the chair. He ran his hand over his face from forehead to chin and then started rubbing the back of his neck.

"Billy Ray, Charlene's pregnant."

I guessed I was supposed to be upset about that news, but I wasn't. I was gonna have a baby. I never thought I could have no baby!

I smiled at Mr. Green's unhappy face. "We gonna have a baby!" I started laughing. I was happier than I had been in the whole last year. My Charlene was still in the local jail where I could see her and we was gonna have a baby. We had two things to celebrate in the new year.

The lawyer looked at me with one eyebrow raised. "You aren't a bright one, are you, Billy Ray?" I guessed he was insulting me but I didn't care much.

"Billy Ray, try to understand what I am going to tell you. Sit."

We sat facing each other. Big Dog came and lay down between us.

Mr. Green clasped his hands together and took a big breath.

"Charlene is going to trial in January. The prosecution will say she is a liar, a whore, and a killer. Tell me, Billy Ray, is she a liar?"

"Yes."

"Is she a whore?"

I shifted uncomfortably in my chair. "Yes," I whispered.

"Is she a killer?"

"Yes."

The lawyer clapped his hands like he was applauding me. He smirked while he did it.

"Very good! The defendant's own lover admits she is a liar, a whore, and a killer!"

I hung my head.

Mr. Green slapped me lightly twice on my left cheek with his right palm. I looked up.

"We have no question of guilt," he said loudly staring past my head as if there was a crowd behind me. "No one thinks Ms. Charlene is not guilty of homicide. But is she guilty of homicide in the first degree?" Mr. Green looked back at me.

"I don't know what first degree is."

"Premeditated murder, Billy Ray."

"Premeditated?"

"Planned, Billy Ray, planned and carried out with full understanding of what she was doing. Like planning to get pregnant so as the jury will feel sorry for her and the baby."

"But Charlene ain't in her right mind, Mr. Green. She wasn't since the day the old man moved in and she still doesn't have a clue who she is or who I am."

Mr. Green smiled crookedly. "Is that what you think, Billy Ray? Do you think that's what the jury's going to think when they find out Charlene also gave sexual favors to the guard on duty in order to have the opportunity to sleep with you?"

I felt a black cloud moving back in over my life at those words. Sexual favors, sexual favors.

I could barely speak. "What sexual favors?"

"Blow jobs, Billy Ray, blow jobs. The kind of favors that guards turn their backs on goings on in the cell."

I felt the heat rising in the room. It came to me that I almost didn't mind her giving a blow job to the officer because she wouldn't be kissing him at the same time and he wouldn't be getting her pregnant. The baby was mine.

"No one would have ever known if she hadn't gotten pregnant, Billy."

"I didn't ever think about her getting pregnant. She never got pregnant the whole two years time we was together alone in the house."

"You all never used any birth control in those two years?"

"I never used nothing. I never saw Charlene use nothing. We wanted to have a baby, so we could be a family."

Mr. Green looked pained. "This just gets worse and worse, Billy Ray. Charlene had what is called an IUD, something inside her to keep her from getting pregnant. She had the doctor take it out when she visited him a month after she was arrested. So, why do you think she did that?" I couldn't follow what he was talking about. I just shook my head.

Mr. Green grabbed my head between his hands.

"Look at me, Billy Ray. Not only did Charlene give blow jobs to the jailer to get sex with you, she only had sex with you to get pregnant. If the jailer hadn't been caught in the act and if the doctor hadn't given us the report about the IUD removal, the jury might damn well have felt sorry for her."

I wanted to block my ears with the flat of my hands and start singing so I couldn't hear what he had to say.

"And that's not all, Billy Ray!" Mr. Green might as well have been the prosecutor for all the bad things he was telling me about Charlene. "Charlene told the jailer she would do anything to have the chance to hold her Sweet Billy Ray in her arms again like it was in the old days with you, her, and Big Dog all curled up together in your bed with the patchwork quilt she made from old cloth you had found."

"Did you ever tell her about that, Billy Ray? Did you?"

I shook my head. "No," I said softly, "I never told her about our life together once she asked who I was."

Mr. Green reached over and put his hand on my knee. "She remembers everything, Billy Ray. Everything and she pretends to you that she can't remember a thing. She slipped up, Billy Ray. She slipped up because she wanted to get pregnant and get sympathy in court. She is totally sane and totally in control. She's a psychopath, Billy Ray, and the jury is going to give her the death penalty, baby or no baby.

He turned to me when he got to the door.

"She's a liar, Billy Ray. A liar, a whore, a killer.....and a liar."

****

Mr. Green was right about Charlene. She was a liar, but she was a liar who wanted to be with me. She was a liar and a whore but she only gave the jailer a blow job and she didn't let him screw her. She wanted to be able to make love with me, have a baby with just me. Is it wrong to lie to do that? Is it wrong to lie to forget your past? Is it wrong to kill to protect your future? Is it wrong to lie to make someone happy? I wondered if I had gone to church I would know more about what was right or what was wrong. It was getting all blurry to me and if I didn't know, maybe Charlene didn't know. I trusted her heart and her love for me. I went back to the jail but this time the new jailer set a chair on the outside of the cell for me.

"Did you do that with the guard so you could see me, Charlene?"

Charlene bit her fingernail. "It wasn't nothing, Billy Ray."

"Did you only let me make love to you to have a baby?"

Charlene shrugged.

"Did you know who I was this whole time you said you didn't?"

Charlene's gaze shifted to her thumbnail. She was more nervous than I had ever seen her before. "I knew who you were," she whispered softly.

"Why, then, Charlene? Why did you say you didn't?"

I looked through the bars at her and for the first time in knowing Charlene, I saw tears in her eyes. I realized she had never cried before. Not when I came back from my time in jail and not when they took her away.

"I thought if I told you I didn't know you, then you would go away."

I felt like she had slapped me through the bars. "You wanted me to go away?

"I knew I was going to go to prison for a long, long time. I wanted you to forget me and go back to our little home up on the hill." She looked dreamily over at the wall where there were only grainy grey bricks to see. "I could see you in my mind, you with Big Dog running in the woods and you making the biscuits I showed you how to make a dozen times and you still make them flat."

She looked back at me. "I can do that in my mind, Billy Ray. I can make our life right here in my mind." Her voiced changed and took on a harder edge. "Then you came back to visit me, over and over again, and you ruined my dream. You were happy in my dream and then you came to the jail, miserable and desperate. You made me have to make you happy here instead and give you the baby you wanted before they took me away from you forever."

Charlene turned away from me and I heard her say, "You've killed me, Billy Ray. You've killed me."

****

"Why do you think she is telling you that you killed her, Billy Ray?" Mr. Green was asking me.

I was trying to understand. "Because if I had left her alone, she could have her dream of me being happy all the time and now I have made her unhappy because she knows I ain't happy..." I couldn't make it sound like any kind of sense.

The lawyer grunted. "No, Billy Ray, you are believing her very inventive story. She pretended not to know you so she would look nuts to a jury and get off with an insanity plea. She doesn't care about you or her unborn baby."

"But she killed the old man for us."

"She killed the old man because she was tired of dealing with him and didn't want the police to find out where she was hiding, Billy Ray."

"She loves me, Mr. Green. I know it. I can feel it. You can't live with a woman a whole two years and not know if she loves you."

Mr. Green laughed at me. "Most people live all their lives with a woman and never know her."

I felt my cheeks burning. "She's innocent, Mr. Green."

"Innocent? What the hell is she innocent of?" Mr. Green slammed his fist down on the case file that he had brought to the house with him. "I am her damned defense attorney and I, for the life of me, can't think of one defense angle to go to court with. She's made a fool of you and she is going to make a fool of me."

I watched him gather his case file and his coat and head for the door.

"Aren't you even going to try and save her, Mr. Green?"

Mr. Green turned at the door and pointed his finger at me.

"You, lover boy, come up with some reason for anyone on that jury to feel sorry for that girl and I'll do my best."

****

Mr. Green entered an insanity plea for Charlene and then the clock started ticking toward the new year. I visited Charlene every day but it wasn't the same as it was before. I couldn't make her smile any more and she looked weary. She was right. I should have gone away and let her pretend we were the happy family on the hill. I was hurting her daily and I watched her get paler and weaker each time I visited. I brought her candies and old magazines and papers I found in people's trash, just to keep her mind off of things. But, she didn't seem to show much interest in anything. Since I wasn't allowed in her cell any more, I couldn't hold her in my arms or kiss her real good. Besides, she had morning sickness all the time and barely could keep any food down.

"Charlene?" I asked her one evening. "How far back do you remember?"

"I remember you coming up to me on the tracks. I remember you taking me home."

"You don't remember what you did over in Bald Eagle?"

She shook her head. "I really don't remember that, Billy Ray. I know you will probably think me a liar, but I just remember standing on the tracks wanting to go home, well, to a place I could call home, when you came and took me there."

"If you couldn't remember being in Bald Eagle, then why would you kill the old man over what happened there?"

Charlene's face turned dark. "Since when are you a goddamned lawyer, Billy Ray? Get the hell out!"

That is when I had my first flicker of doubt that Charlene was anything liked I hoped she was. If she didn't remember the old man, why would she have killed him for me? Why? And if she didn't kill him for me, why did she kill him?

****

Mr. Green spent the evening up on the hill with me.

"I told you, Billy Ray, she killed the man so he wouldn't turn her in to the police."

I shook my head vehemently. "You might as well be the prosecutor, Mr. Green. You seem to believe everything he says about Charlene."

"I do believe everything he says about Charlene. Sometimes defense attorneys have guilty clients, Billy Ray, and there ain't nothing we can do about it except lose the case as gracefully as possible."

"I ain't giving up on Charlene that easy. I know she's changed toward me since I knowed she was lying, but, I still...." I couldn't even finish talking because I knew I sounded stupid.

"Why don't you take Charlene's advice, Billy Ray?" the lawyer asked gently, patting my hand like a child. "Why don't you just stay up here with Big Dog and pretend Charlene was never here."

"What about my baby on the way?"

Mr. Green pursed his lips and then exhaled loudly through them.

"Do you really know it's your baby, Billy Ray? Do you really know she didn't do something more than oral sex with that jailer? Hell, even if the

baby is yours, Billy Ray, the courts wouldn't see you fit to raise an infant alone. I don't mean to insult you none, Billy Ray, but you don't make much money sweeping streets and you won't even have a questionable woman like Charlene in your life to be a mother to that baby. What the courts are bound to do is let Charlene give birth to that baby and then find it a decent home."

I felt sick to my stomach. My baby was going to be raised by someone else and it would still be just me and Big Dog.

****

I came home the next evening after work and Big Dog was dead. Big Dog was lying right in front of the door. He didn't bark. He didn't raise his head and when I pounded on him, it just made a dull thud. I lay sideways on the floor next to Big Dog's head and tried to pry his stiff jaw open with my hands. Then I pressed my nose to his and laid there until I finally fell asleep. I near froze to death on the cold floor that night.

Morning came and Big Dog was just as dead as he was the night before and I had a bad cough. I opened the front door and grabbed Big Dog's back legs and hauled him out on the porch. I had no idea what I was going to do with his body with the ground frozen solid and a foot-high layer of snow over it. I dragged Big Dog down the steps and then I decided to pull him across the road and onto the site of the old burned down house. I piled snow over him and on the top of the little mound, I made a cross with some pine tree branches. I still didn't believe in God all that well, but I loved Big Dog and thought he deserved some kind of grave.

I was feeling so sad I wondered why no tears were coming out of my eyes and then I realized when I saw Big Dog dead, I didn't cry at all. I wondered if I had so much bad luck that I was tired of crying about things. I wondered if that's why Charlene never cried. Was she as coldhearted as everyone said or was she all cried out?

I spent that night trying to figure out what had happened to me as well as Charlene after everything went wrong. I remembered that I once lived alone on that mountain with no Charlene and no Big Dog. Life was all right. I don't remember being unhappy. Maybe, I kind of wished I had what other people had but I didn't know no different, so I didn't think I had it so bad. But, then I got Big Dog and then Charlene and now I missed what I never missed before. I wondered whether having love was worth all the trouble of losing it.

I still didn't know the answer by morning, but I did know that I wanted it back.

III

I went to visit Charlene that evening. I wondered if she would even want to see me after she told me to get the hell out. Did she hate me or love me?

I arrived after dinnertime and the police officer let me into the room next to her cell. Charlene was lying on her cot facing the wall.

I said real quiet, "Charlene?"

She didn't respond.

"Charlene? It's Billy Ray. Are you gonna talk to me?"

She moved enough to let me know she was awake.

"I'm sorry I asked you so many questions last time, honey. I love you, Charlene."

Charlene pushed the covers back and rolled over on her cot. She looked like hell, but she was smiling. She ran across the cold floor barefooted and kissed me through the bars.

"I got something to show you, Billy Ray." She handed me a piece of notepaper."

I looked at the writing scratched on it and asked her what it said.

"Cheryl Wiggington. Fort Hanley."

I looked up from the paper to her excited face. "Is this you?"

Charlene laughed. Laughed! "It's me! I remember who I am!'

Her face saddened a little. "I remember Bald Eagle. I remember why I was there and what I did." She didn't look up at me.

I suddenly felt Mr. Green should be here.

"Charlene, you need to tell all this to Mr. Green. It might help you in the trial. Okay?"

Charlene nodded.

"I'll go get him right away. Don't you forget anything, honey, while I'm gone." I put a finger through the bar, lifted her chin and kissed her lips. When I looked into her blue eyes, I saw me in them.

****

Mr. Green, Charlene and I sat in the talking room and he started a tape recorder so none of us would forget what was said that night.

Mr. Green started.

"Charlene? Can you tell me your whole name? Your real name?"

She cleared her throat and spoke in such a little voice, Mr. Green had to ask her to speak more loudly for the tape recording.

She tried again and this time her voice was clear. "Cheryl Wiggington."

"Date of Birth?"

"January 1, 1990."

"So you are twenty-one years old, turning twenty-two in January?"

Charlene twisted a napkin between her fingers. I bit my tongue.

"Uh-huh."

"Where were you born, Charlene?"

"In Fort Hanley, Arkansas."

Mr. Green leaned back in his chair. "Tell me what you remember from your childhood there, Charlene."

Charlene frowned.

"I don't remember very much at all. I remember a little house. It was blue with white shutters. I remember a big ugly tree in the yard with a rope swing on it that I loved a lot. I remember the kitchen. It was yellow. I

remember my mother. She had long blonde hair, and long fingernails, and her teeth stuck out funny and they hurt sometimes when she kissed me. I had a little brother and sister."

"And your father?"

"I didn't have a father." Charlene spoke that rather angrily and I wondered what made her so mad.

"Dead?"

"I don't know."

Mr. Green was observing her very carefully.

"When do you remember being with your family, Charlene?"

Charlene twisted the napkin into a snake and played with it on the desk. She seemed to drift off so Mr. Green asked her again.

"Maybe when I was six. I remember the school building down the block but I don't remember being in it."

Mr. Green asked what she next remembered.

Charlene looked over at me and then back at Mr. Green.

"I remember being cold and hungry and the old man giving me money in Bald Eagle for some food."

Mr. Green got that look on his face like he didn't trust what she was saying.

"Are you telling me you remember nothing from the time you were six until the time you were...let me think...about nineteen years old?

Charlene started ripping her snake into shreds on the table. I leaned forward to calm her down but Mr. Green signaled me to leave her alone.

"Charlene? Do you remember nothing about sleeping with men for money? Sleeping with that old man 'who gave you money for food?' Ripping him off?"

Charlene shook her head back and forth, back and forth.

Mr. Green pressed on. "Don't you even remember the children you had?"

Charlene's body started jerking in a strange manner and she began madly mutilating the little pieces of snake she had deposited on the table *until she started making noises that I couldn't identify as human. At that point, Mr. Green started getting scared and he called for the officers to come and get Charlene. When they touched her, she started thrashing around so wildly it took three of them to pin her to the floor and then she bit the arm of one of them and he yelped and another of them slammed her head to the floor with his forearm and held it there while they called for an ambulance to come and take her to the hospital.*

I felt horrible for Charlene, to see her being treated like an animal, and I lied down beside her on the floor while we waited for the medical people to show up. I looked over at her face held tight to the floor under the uniformed arm and it was then I saw she was laughing.

I got up and left the room.

****

The ambulance came and took her away. Mr. Green and I sat back down in the talking room.

"She was laughing, Mr. Green. Laughing."

Mr. Green smiled just a bit it seemed.

"People laugh for lots of reasons, Billy Ray. Sometimes because they're happy but sometimes because they're sad and can't cry. Sometimes they go completely hysterical when they can't express themselves in a way that anyone can understand."

I guessed that made sense. Charlene laughed so little in our time together, it was strange to see her doing it at that particular moment.

Mr. Green calmed me down.

"She obviously was very upset about the loss of those children for whatever reason they aren't with her today. We will get to the bottom of this, Billy Ray. We have her name now, a birthdate, and the place she grew up. Maybe we will finally get some answers."

I nodded tiredly. I hoped he was right. Suddenly, it seemed Mr. Green was believing more in Charlene than me.

****

It turned out Mr. Green was right as rain. The answers showed up just a week later at the doorstep of the State Hospital in the forms of Mrs. Wiggington and her son and daughter. Mrs. Wiggington was as Charlene said. Very blonde (but her hair was now short), long fingernails, and some really bad teeth that made me hope she wouldn't kiss me for any reason. She was crying like a baby and her son and daughter kept hugging her and telling her it was okay.

Actually, I first laid eyes on the family when they got to the waiting room outside Charlene's room. We were on a locked floor and a police guard stood in front of Charlene's room twenty-four hours a day. Until they showed up, only me and Mr. Green came to see Charlene.

Mr. Green stood up when the Wiggingtons came into the waiting room. He had been expecting them.

"Mrs. Wiggington? Please sit down."

She plopped down right in the middle of the sofa, each of her children sitting down beside her. She sniffled some more.

"Did you bring the papers, Mrs. Wiggington?" asked Mr. Green.

She fished in her large purse and pulled out an official looking document and a newspaper clipping. She handed them over to Mr. Green who studied them for a long time and said nothing. Finally, he looked up.

"Well, this is most interesting and may answer a lot of our questions about Charlene."

I was itching to know what the papers said and Mr. Green handed them over to me. He told me what each one was. One had her name on it and the date that she was born. It had Fort Hanley Community Hospital written in fancy lettering across the top. I put that one down carefully on the table and looked at the newspaper clipping. It had a picture of a pretty little blond girl and underneath it Mr. Green told me was written "Missing: Cheryl Bettina Wiggington." I looked up at Mrs. Wiggington. I wondered what was in the rest of the story.

Mr. Green looked over at the blonde woman. She blew her nose.

"Can I ask you to tell us what happened to Charlene, uh, Cheryl? Is it all right if I record what you tell me?" He pulled his little tape recorder out and set it on the table between them.

Mrs. Wiggington looked a bit flustered at the tape recorder.

"Please, remember, Mrs. Wiggington, Cheryl is going to trial. Anything said about her is part of evidence for the defense or prosecution."

Mrs. Wiggington started crying again but she managed a nod.

Mr. Green hit the record button.

"Can you state your full name for the record?"

"Mrs. Lucinda May Wiggington."

"And your date of birth?"

"July 31st...," she giggled a little here and I remember what Mr. Green said about hysteria, "uh, 1974."

I felt kind of strange being only a few years younger than Charlene's mother. I never thought about Charlene and mine's ages until then.

"Tell us what happened to Cheryl."

Mrs. Wiggington stopped laughing and started crying again.

"Well, we adopted Cheryl when she was just a baby and then when Cheryl was five," she shook her head at this, "my husband left me. Where he went, I never knew. Then a year later, Cheryl was just starting into first grade and on the second day of school she left the building...someone saw her walking toward the flagpole out in front of the school...and then she just never arrived home. First, we thought she had got lost and then when it got dark, we started panicking. My first thought was my husband had come back and stole her away and I told the police that."

"Did they check him out?" asked Mr. Green.

"Yeah, they said they did. They said they found him but they wouldn't tell me where. They said he couldn't have taken her and that she has never been seen with him since. I always thought it strange, though, that he never called me to ask about Cheryl. Never."

"Did any other suspects ever turn up?"

"Well, yes, they had one really good suspect. They said there was a pedophile who was a suspect in a missing child case three years ago in another town who had been seen in Fort Hanley around the time Cheryl went missing. They said they checked him out as thoroughly as they could but they never found evidence linking him to her disappearance."

Mrs. Wiggington paused and stared blankly around the room.

"And?" encouraged Mr. Green.

Mrs. Wiggington gave a little soft snort.

"And nothing. Just nothing. Cheryl never was found. I always thought my husband had taken her and hidden her away so I could never see her again." She burst into tears.

Her daughter leaned over and hugged her.

"But we found her Ma! We found her!"

Mrs. Wiggington grinned and sniffed and said, "Yeah, yeah, we finally found her!"

Mr. Green reached over and turned the tape recorder off.

"Go on. Go meet your daughter."

The family went on in to see Charlene and I wished I could have been there with them, but it wouldn't have been right.

Mr. Green stood up and put the tape recorder into his pocket and gave it a pat.

"We may have our miracle, Billy Ray. It's called post-traumatic stress disorder. PTSD. We got ourselves a whole new ballgame."

Mr. Green actually gave me a hug as he left the room. I hadn't seen him so happy since he started working on Charlene's case.

PTSD. Sounded a lot like those sexual diseases Charlene got before. I hoped this one would do her some good.

****

I saw Charlene a few more times before the trial started in January. Just before the big day, I finally met the family at a little birthday celebration for Charlene in her hospital room. She got a real sweet "daughter" card from her Mama and two "sister" cards from Pammy and Donny, her siblings. I gave her a "sweetheart" card. She had a whole tray full of relationships sitting in front of her.

Charlene laughed and smiled that day like she had just learned what it was like to be happy. I sat in my chair and enjoyed her new found family and my new family . Yes, my new family! I got me a mother-in-law and a little brother and little sister and our new baby would have a Grandma and an aunt and an uncle! And they didn't seem to care much that I was black. They never even batted an eye about that. They gave me hugs and didn't call me ugly or stupid or any other bad names.

Charlene was twenty-two years old that day. The first day of the year was starting off just fine. We was all together in this, one big happy family and Charlene had a lawyer who believed in her. Well, at least he believed a little something about her. He at least believed now she could be crazy and that was good enough for me.

III

January 5th - First day of the trial

I started checking off the date book I had bought at Ben Franklins when the trial started. I wanted to know exactly when we started into this part of our lives and when we would end it. The trial was going to take more than half a day now that Mr. Green was ready to fight for Charlene's life. I planned to be in that courtroom every day so Charlene would know I loved her. The prosecutor gave what they call an opening statement and I just wanted to close my ears through the whole thing. He said every hurtful thing he could about Charlene including her being a whore, a liar, and a psychopath which he explained was someone who didn't care about nobody but herself.

"That woman," he shouted pointing over at Charlene, "only looks out for herself. She is a true psychopath in that she either finds someone useful or she finds them in the way. Mr. Doe, as we must called our unidentified victim of Ms. Wiggington's anger, found himself among the useful when the defendant came upon him in Bald Eagle. He gave her money and what he didn't give her, she stole from him. Then she killed him when he got in her way.

Mr. Dawson, the prosecutor was balding and fat. But, he moved quickly and spun around to point his finger straight at me.

"When Ms. Wiggington went on the lam from the police, she found "this" man to be useful to her. He gave her shelter; a hiding place far off in the mountains where no one would find her. Well, at least that is what she thought until John Doe showed up across the way."

He turned back toward the jury and grandly gestured, his hands stretching out in large arcs. "And, then? What did she do to this man?" He pointed back at me. "This man, who loved her, fed her, sheltered her, and was willing to take the blame for the killing of his neighbor just to save her from prison?"

He dropped his hands and turned slowly back toward the jury. His arms now hung limply at his sides.

"This man," he said quietly, "she denied even knowing. When he came to give her his support, she pretended not to recognize him. Why? Because she was working on her insanity plea."

Mr. Dawson patted his sides and shook his head.

The prosecutor then pointed again at Charlene. His voice was no longer tired and weak.

"This woman, this psychopath, this liar, this whore, this user of people, " his voiced boomed out and echoed off the walls. "This woman was still to play one more card to try to get away with her premeditated murder of Mr. Doe. She bribed the police guard with sex in order to impregnate herself by Mr. Hutchins and gain sympathy from a jury; she is trying to play on your feelings about putting a pregnant woman on death row and leaving a baby motherless! How cruel and coldhearted it is to use an unborn baby to keep oneself out of the gas chamber!"

His voice went on but I lost track of what he said after the part about Charlene using me just to make a baby. Mr. Green had told me that was what she was doing and that it would backfire on her in court. But, ever since the Wiggingtons had showed up in town, he had changed his tune, telling me maybe Charlene hadn't really been thinking about the court case when she bribed the jailer to let me be with her. I tried to think back to see if her wanting to have sex every night in the jail was anything but her wanting to love me and I can't remember anything she did to make it seem like she was just using me. Everything was the same in our lovemaking as it had been at the house except for the bars surrounding it. I only wished she had called me Sweet Billy Ray the way she used to every time we made love in our bed.

****

I asked Mr. Green what he thought when we broke for lunch.

"Why would she tell the police officer she wanted to be with Sweet Billy Ray but never call me that when we was making love in the cell?"
Mr. Green just shook his head.
"I ain't no psychiatrist, Billy Ray. I can't say why she would do exactly this or that."
Mr. Green smiled at me.
"Billy Ray, you have to start thinking positively now. We got ourselves a defense and you have to support Charlene one-hundred percent."
He leaned forward and spoke in a hushed voice across my pepperoni pizza plate.
"The prosecutor has to prove Charlene is a psychopath who planned this murder with total free will. He has to prove that she knew what she was doing before she did it and she worked to cover up her crime after she did it because she knew what she did was wrong. Psychopaths are smart and they know right from wrong. This is what his argument is going to be."
I could follow that. I had been starting to understand this psychopath stuff from everyone telling me that Charlene was one of them.
"Now, I have a different thing to prove to the jury. I have to prove to them that Charlene was crazy at the time of the murder; that something drove her to do it that she had no control over, and her behavior before and after the murder only supports that she was out of her mind when she killed Mr. Doe."
Mr. Green pushed himself back to his upright position and got up from the table.
"You just watch my opening statment this afternoon. I'll make Mr. Dawson look like one unfeeling bastard."
I watched Mr. Green as he walked away and wondered if he lied and changed his tune as much as Charlene. Maybe lawyers weren't so different from the clients they represented. Now It wss hard to know who to trust.

****

Mr. Green sure did turn things upside down. Just before lunch I could see the jury members looking at Charlene like she was some kind of poisonous insect. By the end of the afternoon, they were looking at her as if she were a lost puppy they wanted to adopt and take home to their children.

Mr. Green didn't do all that loud yelling and pointing and wild gesturing that Mr. Dawson did. He talked quietly and firmly and made Mr. Dawson look like one of those snake oil salesmen trying to fool his audience into buying something they don't need.

The defense attorney got up quietly from the table and took his glasses off. He laid them carefully on top of the case files. He walked towards the jury and looked them over from left to right. He looked into all of their eyes and let them look into his.

He started with a statement.

"A terrible event has occurred in a place where nothing like this has happened in the last decades we can remember. No one has been murdered in their home for reasons unknown and never have we had a woman in this town on the stand fighting for her life."

He paused.

"We find ourselves at quite a loss. We want justice done for this victim and we want to have mercy for this woman if we find any reason for it. But, we are about to tread into the most confusing arena of our lives. We do not have to decide if a homicide occurred. Ms. Wiggington does not deny it occurred. We do not have to decide who committed this homicide because Ms. Wiggington does not deny she is the one who killed Mr. Doe. But we must solve a very unusual puzzle in order to be able to say that justice for one death demands the death of another. We don't know what drove Mr. Doe to take up residence directly across from someone the prosecutor, Mr. Dawson, claims robbed him of his money, and we don't know what drove Ms. Wiggington to become so desperate to be free of this man's presence that she would be driven to kill him to achieve that freedom."

I could see right here that Mr. Green was making the jury think that maybe it wasn't as simple as Mr. Dawson told them it was.

Mr. Green looked over the jury again.

"Mr. Dawson says Ms. Wiggington is a liar and that makes her a psychopath."

He laughed.

"I hope what he says is not true and that he is a very poor specimen of a psychiatrist because if what he says is so, then you," and he paused to let his eyes roll over each and every jury member, "You and I and the judge here..."

The judge raised an eyebrow of warning at him.

"Sorry, Your Honor," apologized Mr. Green, "But all of us here would be labeled psychopaths for telling a lie now and then to keep our wives or husbands from killing us and to keep our bosses from firing us." The jury laughed.

Mr. Green looked very serious again.

"Yes, Ms. Wiggington has lied. She has lied quite a lot. Sometimes she didn't lie but she just didn't offer the truth. In spite of these failings, Mr. Hutchins lived happily with this woman for two years, never feeling misled, never feeling abused. In fact," Mr. Green gently waved in my direction, "Mr. Hutchins thought so highly of his companion that he was willing to go to jail for her because he believed she could not have killed without reason; that she could not have been so coldhearted and therefore he could not be so coldhearted as to believe her to be so."

I didn't know until now that was why I was willing to go to jail for Charlene but he put it so nicely and it made so much sense that I felt good about what I did and I felt good about Charlene.

Mr. Green nailed Mr. Dawson again.

"Mr. Dawson must prove to you that Ms. Wiggington had a clear motive to kill Mr. Doe that was purely for selfish interests and that she was entirely in her right mind when she decided to do so. He cannot merely make up stories about Ms. Wiggington that he 'guesses' might be why she

killed Mr. Doe; he must have proof of her exact state of mind and irrefutable evidence that she knew why she shot Mr. Doe on that fateful morning when Mr. Hutchins left her alone to go into town for his cigarettes and some candy for his lady."

Mr. Green finally raised his voice, but he didn't shout. He just raised it so there was no way to ignore what he would say next.

"Why, ladies and gentlemen of the jury, is the only question which must be answered fully and satisfactorily. Let Mr. Dawson prove why Ms. Wiggington took Mr. Doe's life and after he has proven why, you can decide if that answer to this riddle is evil enough to put Ms. Wiggington to death."

Mr. Green walked back to his desk and put his glasses back on. He glanced down at his case file and tapped it with his forefinger.

"This, ladies and gentlemen, is my exploration into Ms. Wiggington's life. By the time this trial is over, you will understand exactly what caused Ms. Wiggington to risk all the good things she finally had in her life - a home, a loving man - why she would risk losing all those beautiful things to rid herself of the man across the street, a man who represented another who had taken her from her family, a man she thought was that man who had destroyed her life. When you finally understand what made her commit such a horrible crime as the taking of another human's life, you will find Ms. Wiggington not guilty by reason of insanity."

I got it and I hoped the jury did to. Charlene killed that man because that PTSD made her confuse him with another bad man. I felt relief wash over me.

The afternoon was over and when I went to sleep that night, I dreamed Charlene was back where she belonged in our bed and Big Dog was panting quietly nearby on the floor. I hoped she was dreaming the same thing.

January 6 - Day Two

It was so darn cold today I wished my truck would start. I put gas back in it but now I think the battery has gone dead. I hope I can get Mr. Green to come up here and jumpstart it with his truck, but for now I have to get dressed, so I can meet the Wiggingtons in town and I can get into the courtroom.

I almost wished I hadn't made it to court today. The room was filled with lots of curious people, maybe everyone who lived in town who could get off work and those who didn't have to work. Nothing bad happened but then nothing good happened either. I fell asleep a dozen times and when I woke up I saw the jury was napping too. What the lawyers was talking about today was some legal stuff that didn't make too much sense to me at all. I guess the spectators were disappointed as well because they looked pretty bored. The only part that made me pay attention real good was when the doctor took the stand for the prosecution. Mrs. Wiggington was sitting next to me at that time and she squeezed my hand real hard and woke me up.

Mr. Dawson asked the doctor questions about Charlene's health, like did she have any serious illnesses, was she dying of anything, and was there any medical issues that would do harm to her mind.

The doctor shook his head.

"No, sir, Ms. Wiggington is in good health. She has normal blood pressure, normal pulse, a normal blood cell count, no sugar; nothing unusual or unexpected presented itself in her exam. She is a healthy young woman of twenty-two."

Mr. Dawson nodded in agreement.

"Did you do an internal exam as well? A female exam?"

"Yes, sir, I did."

"Can you tell us what your findings were?"

The doctor shifted uncomfortably in his seat. Mrs. Wiggington tightened her grip on my hand.

"Well, sir, it was clear from scars from perineal tears that she had birthed at least couple of babies vaginally." At that, the jury exchanged looks.
"Go on, doctor."
"Also a history of STD's - sexually transmitted diseases. She's healthy now but she had been treated for some diseases in her past."
Mr. Dawson looked satisfied. He started towards his table and then he stopped and looked back.
"But, to be perfectly fair, Doctor, did you do any x-rays to see if the defendant might have been the subject of physical abuse?"
The doctor nodded.
"Yes, sir. I did do x-rays. There are no signs of healed broken bones in her body."
"No more questions, Your Honor."
The prosecutor look more than satisfied now. He left the jury wondering what Charlene had been doing to get pregnant so many times and get diseases so often. I wanted to punch the prosecutor in his smug face.
Mr. Green stood up.
"One question, Doctor. Did you do any CT scans to see if Ms. Wiggington had suffered any brain injury?"
The doctor looked surprised.
"No, sir, they never asked me to do that."
"Thank you, Doctor. That's all."

****

January 7 - Day 3

I hated this day right from the start. I don't know where Mr. Dawson found all those men from Eagle Rock but it seemed like the whole population of males from that town came into the courtroom.
"Did you have sex with the defendant?"
"Yes, sir. Her, over there, in the blue dress." He pointed at Charlene.

"Did you have sex with the defendant?"

"Yes, sir. I gave her," he pointed at Charlene, "twenty dollars and she gave me a blow job in my car."

"Did you have sex with the defendant?"

"Well, I sure as hell 'would' have if the bitch, sorry, Your Honor, if the defendant hadn't ripped me off. She took my money, pulled down my pants behind the liquor store and when I had them around my knees, she took off running."

I heard people stifling their laughing. I wanted to laugh myself and then I felt bad for feeling like I wanted to.

"Did you have sex with the defendant?"

"Did you have sex with the defendant?"

"Did you have sex with the defendant?"

I left the courtroom when I couldn't listen to that question any more. I wanted to go back to believing she was a virgin when she came to me and that we didn't have no one else ever knowing what was between us. I sat out in the hallway until lunchtime when the door opened and the courtroom emptied for the noontime recess.

Mr. Green found me and steered me towards the cafeteria.

I looked at him and asked what else had happened since I left the courtroom.

He just shook his head and told me, "More of the same, more of the same." When we got to the lunch line, I didn't want nothing to eat. Mr. Green bought me some vegetable soup and tried to make me drink it. I felt like throwing up. I couldn't even bring the stuff to my mouth.

We didn't talk at all during lunch. What was Mr. Green gonna say to me? "Sorry everyone has slept with your girl? Sorry I missed my opportunity?" I began to wonder if he did. Maybe that's why he was trying harder now.

I saw Mrs. Wiggington across the lunchroom. She didn't look like she was eating too good herself. Her daughter was worse than just a killer. She was the whore of whores.

Mr. Green cuffed me on the head to knock me out of my stupor.
"That was before you, Billy Ray, before you. Don't forget that."
Yeah, I guess. If one could forget she blew the jailer.
The afternoon went a bit better because Mr. Green was calling the shots.
He got some other men of Eagle Rock on the stand and they had some
nicer things to say about Charlene.
"I thought she was a sweet girl. She seemed confused. I didn't even want to
sleep with her but she insisted she needed the money."
"I don't think she had a place to sleep. She looked hungry. I gave her five
dollars and she went down on me. Five dollars." The man looked around
at the courtroom's expressions. "Hey, it was all I had that week."
Finally, one man said, "She didn't even seem to know her own name. I
thought she might be on drugs but I didn't see any track marks on her
arms. I thought then maybe she was crazy."
So the jury left the day knowing that Charlene was a whore but not
knowing what made her one. Mr. Green said it was a win for the defense.
Charlene may have been whore but she was hungry, homeless, and maybe
crazy. The best part was when I heard that she didn't know her name.
Maybe Charlene was telling the truth about not remembering things.

****

January 8 - Day Four

This morning the prosecutor destroyed all the good things Mr. Green had
the jury thinking when they went home last night.
The first man on the stand said she tried to kill him with a knife when he
asked her to leave the motel room he'd gotten himself for the whole night.
The second man said she not only stole his money, but she stole all his
wife's jewelry from the bedside stand.
The third man said she tried to blackmail him after she found out he was
on the city council.

Finally, someone said they saw Charlene with Mr. Doe a few days before she disappeared from Eagle Rock.

Mr. Dawson was very interested in this particular story. His face lit up and he looked over at the jury to make sure they were awake and paying attention.

"Mr. Clemens," he asked, "You own a motel?"

"Yes, sir. I own the Lighthouse Motel on Sandy Avenue.

"How much does it cost to rent a room there?"

"For the night?"

There was laughter scattered about the room and Mr. Clemens smiled out at the audience.

"Yes, sir, for a night."

"That would be $26 if you were by yourself and $35 for two if you didn't lie and sneak the second person in." Mr. Clemens seemed to enjoy entertaining the people in the room.

"Did you ever rent a room to Mr. Doe?"

"Well, I don't know if he was the same man you are referring to but by all the descriptions he is. I don't recall what he wrote down in the book and I don't keep no records past the end of the month. If the police ain't come calling by then, I figger the person ain't done anything all that bad."

Mr. Dawson smiled toward the witness stand.

"And this man that looked like Mr. Doe? How long did he stay?"

Mr. Clemens squinched up his left eye and looked up to some far away place off to his side.

"Well, I am thinking he stayed about four or five days. He wasn't just there for sex. He gave me money for the week and I didn't see much of him until I saw him with the girl. Her." Mr. Clemens pointed over at Charlene.

"And what was he doing with the defendant?"

"He wasn't doing anything with her. She was slapping him all over his head and he was just ducking there against the wall trying to protect

hisself. Then she run off and I never saw her at my motel again. He left before the rent for the week ran out."

"Thank you, Mr. Clemens." He nodded toward Mr. Green. "Your witness, Counselor."

Mr. Green got up and stared at Mr. Clemens until he started squirming in the chair. I thought he was going to make Mr. Clemens say he didn't know if he had really seen Mr. Doe at his motel with Charlene. But, he surprised me.

"Mr. Clemens, Mr. Doe came to your hotel in the day or at night?"

"Daytime, sir. I remember because he came up in the middle of the afternoon. Most of my clients don't show up until they done enough drinking and found their pigeon for the night." Clemens grinned again.

Mr. Green smiled graciously back at him.

"So you were clearheaded yourself when Mr. Doe showed up?"

Mr. Clemens looked flustered and a little angry.

"I don't drink when I work, Mr. Green."

"I am not accusing you of drinking on the job, Mr. Clemens. I am just clarifying to the jury that you were completely sober and the observations you made that day would not be clouded by any kind of alcoholic beverages."

Mr. Clemens sat up in his chair.

"Yes, sir, Mr. Green, the jury can depend on what I saw that day as being exactly what I saw that day."

"He checked in during the afternoon?"

"Yes, sir. Middle of the afternoon. I thought he might have come off the 2 pm Greyhound bus seeing as he had no car and he looked too old to be walking any distance."

"So he didn't have a car with a lot of stuff packed in it like he was moving from here to there."

"No, sir, no car. Just hisself and his bag.

"One bag?"

"Yes, sir. A duffel."

"So he came off a bus...."

"Objection."

"Sustained."

Mr. Green nodded. *"I will rephrase that. Mr. Doe arrived at your motel at around 3 pm in the afternoon with one duffel bag in his possession."*

"Yes, sir, that would be correct."

"And he paid you a week's rent?"

"Yeah, well, sort of. He wasn't all too pleasant about the rate I told him. He complained I was overcharging him and didn't I think Vets deserved a break and how he was an old man and he could drop dead tonight if I didn't give him a place to stay for the money he had."

"So did you give him a break?"

"Yes, sir. I felt kind of sorry for him. He looked damned pitiful. He needed a haircut, and a shower, and his clothes looked like they were glued on him. I asked him how much money he had and he pulled out a wad of bills from his pocket and we counted them together."

"How much did he have?"

"He had seventy-five dollars all together, so I told him he could stay for the week for fifty. I wasn't filling up the rooms anyway."

"So, he moved in for the week?"

Mr. Clemens nodded. *"Yeah, I walked him over to his room and he was a lot more pleasant once he knew he had a place to stay. He even chatted me up while he dumped his bag all over the floor of the motel room."*

"All his worldly possessions?"

"If you could call them that," he laughed.

"Objection!"

"What's your objection, Counselor?"

"Well, Your Honor, where the hell is the defense going with this happy trot down memory lane?"

The judge looked over at Mr. Green. *"Counselor?"*

"Your Honor, the prosecution has opened up the door by bringing this witness in to testify about the relationship between Mr. Doe and Ms.

Wiggington. I allowed without objection to let the witness describe an alleged fight that occurred between the two of them on the premises of his motel. It should be clear to the court that the entire purpose of the prosecution in bringing this particular witness to the stand is to establish motive for the later killing of Mr. Doe by the defendant. I am only trying to assist in establishing that motive."

A smile played on the judge's lips for a moment and then he told Mr. Green to proceed.

Mr. Green turned back to the witness.

"Mr. Dawson, uh, sorry, Mr. Clemens, you were describing your time with Mr. Doe in his room. You were saying he dumped the contents of his duffel bag on the floor of the room in your presence."

"Yeah, he did, but you know, he did it like he didn't even realize I was still standing there."

"Can you describe the contents of the bag?"

Mr. Clemens shrugged.

"Well, it was a lot of clothing like you would expect. That's all."

"Did you see anything other than clothing?"

"Nope."

"Just clothing."

"Yep. Then he started rattling on about the government not paying his disability and I left him alone."

Mr. Green stroked his chin and reviewed what Mr. Clemens had told him.

"So, Mr. Doe gave you fifty dollars for the room of the seventy-five he had. How many days passed before you saw him with Ms. Wiggington?"

"I guess it would be that weekend. He came in on a Wednesday. So, probably three or four."

"So I guess he would have had to spend some of that money on food before the weekend came?"

"Objection! Asking the witness for a conclusion."

"Sustained."

Mr. Green nodded.

"Just one last question, Mr. Clemens. When you saw Ms. Wiggington slapping Mr. Doe on the head in the hallway and run away, did you see her with any money in her hands or any other article of value?"

"No, sir."

"Thank you, Mr. Clemens." He looked at the judge. "I'm finished with this witness."

Mr. Dawson stood up. "One question."

The judge nodded.

"Did you check her pockets, Mr. Clemens?" The courtroom laughed.

Mr. Clemens shook his head. "No, sir, she didn't give me the opportunity!"

"No further questions."

****

When I got to the lunch table, Mr. Green was smiling. I felt angry that he was feeling so good after what that next group of men said about Charlene.

"They said she was a criminal, Mr. Green. They said she was a thief and a blackmailer and she'd tried to hurt them. They made her look worse than just a whore."

"Yeah, Billy Ray, they did that. But, that wasn't the important part of what happened in there today. It was what Mr. Clemens said about Mr. Doe that mattered."

I didn't understand. "He said Charlene beat up Mr. Doe."

Mr. Green actually put down his coffee and laughed.

"Yeah, he did, but what did Charlene get so mad at Mr. Doe for?"

I shrugged. "Seemed to me like he didn't have no money left to pay her for what she gave him."

Mr. Green clapped me on the shoulder.

"You getting pretty smart there, Billy Ray."

I didn't see how I was smart.

"Do you remember Mr. Dawson trying to say how Charlene was ripping off them men and how Mr. Doe probably came out to the Glen to get whatever she took from him back?"

I remembered.

"Do you see how all those men he brought called her a thief so we could believe she robbed Mr. Doe too?"

I could see that.

"Now what the hell do you think Charlene could have taken from that old man at the Lighthouse Motel if all he had was a few dollars left and a bag of rags?"

"I dunno."

"Exactly, Billy Ray. We all dunno and we sure dunno why he would travel all that distance to the Glen to get back the nothing she could have taken off of him."

One other thing bothered me and I had to ask him.

"Are you sure that man was really Mr. Doe?"

Mr. Green grinned widely and leaned close to me.

"I haven't the faintest idea if that is the same man who moved cross the way from you. But, since the prosecution was so excited to make him Mr. Doe, I couldn't see why we shouldn't go along with it. The real Mr. Doe in the fire ain't got no teeth to check for dental records and it's my guess we'll never know who he really is, but if Mr. Dawson wants to make a penniless old drifter into Mr. Doe, I've got no objection! He isn't going to establish much motive that way."

I looked at Mr. Green and I tried to see where he was going.

"But, if Charlene didn't do nothing to the old man and he didn't come to do nothing to her, why would she kill him? Is it cause like you said she thought he was someone else?"

Mr. Green bit his lip and shook his head a few times back and forth.

"That's the million dollar question, Billy Ray. If you can get her to tell you, it would save us a whole lotta work and guessing."

"So, maybe she is just crazy."

"Maybe, Billy Ray. That's for me to make the jury think and if it's a good enough answer for the jury, it's good enough to save Charlene's life."

****

The heating system stopped working on Thursday night, so on Friday morning there was frost collecting on the benches in the courtroom and they canceled court until Monday. They brought Charlene back from the hospital to the jail and I went over to see her. I should have gone to work that day since I didn't have to go to court but I wanted to see Charlene so bad that I went over to the boss and asked him if I could make some money on the weekend. He was nice about it and told me to go on over and see Charlene.

When I got over to the jail, I told the officer I wanted to see Charlene but he told me I would have to come back later, that she was spending the morning with her Mama. I waited a couple of hours and he came back and told me she was now spending the next hours with her sister. I tried again in the evening, but then he told me she said she was too tired to see me.

I didn't go to work Saturday or Sunday neither. I spent both days trying to get in to see Charlene. She was always occupied or tired or visiting with someone else. The police officer finally told me that I was stupid if I didn't get that she just didn't want to see me. I went over to the motel down the block where the Wiggingtons were staying and banged on their door. Mrs. Wiggington let me in. She was still dressed from her visit down at the jail. She gave me a little hug and patted me absentmindedly on the head.

I asked her if she knew what was wrong with Charlene and why she didn't want to see me.

"She's just confused, hon. Give her time."

"Confused? What is she confused about?"

"She isn't sure can love you right now, Sweetie."

I felt like I had all the wind knocked out of me.

"She don't love me no more?" The words felt like dry straw in my mouth.

Mrs. Wiggington pulled me in the door and sat me down on the motel bed. She went to her little refrigerator and got herself a beer. "Want one?" I shook my head. I never drank beer in my whole life.

She came back and sat down beside me and the boozy smell of the beer made me feel sick. Or maybe it was hearing her say Charlene didn't love me. Or maybe it was sitting next to Mrs. Wiggington in her little short skirt that bothered me.

Mrs. Wiggington went right on and told me all about Charlene and their visits.

"Cheryl is real confused, Billy Ray. She told me she didn't want to hurt your feelings but she thinks now she came to stay with you because she couldn't find her way back to us."

"She kind of already told me that."

Mrs. Wiggington nodded and took a long drink of her beer.

"But, she has found her way back to us, Billy Ray. She has her family around her and she is finding it hard to split herself between you and us." "And I don't matter no more?"

Mrs. Wiggington finished off the beer and she seemed a little drunk. "Aw, honey, I'm not saying that. I'm saying that," she seemed to realize she was repeating herself, "what I am saying is she finally can be my little girl again; she doesn't want to be a grown up right now with a man she has to take care of. She just wants to be my baby again."

Maybe there was some sense in that. I didn't say nothing though. I just wanted to hear Mrs. Wiggington tell me about Charlene.

She wanted to tell me about her 'Cheryl' too. She leaned against me and told me how she finally could smile again and how she could start getting back all those years she lost when Charlene went missing. She made me uncomfortable and she made me mad.

"Cheryl is going to have such a wonderful time when we get her out of this little bit o' trouble!"

A little trouble? I was beginning to see where Charlene got her craziness from.

"I am going to take Cheryl home and let her ride on the swing she never got to use. We put it up the week after she went missing, thinking maybe it would draw her home.

Mrs. Wiggington got quiet for a minute. She smiled.

"Huh, maybe that ol' swing really did bring her home, you think, Billy Ray?"

I wasn't really thinking of Charlene at home with her family. I was thinking about Charlene sleeping in another bed far away from me.

"Anyway, I want to bring her home and show Cheryl her room with all her stuffed animals still in it. And I want to walk her to her school and back home again. I want her to eat her dinner with us and I want to say prayers with her before she goes to sleep at night."

I just couldn't listen any more.

"Bye, Mrs. Wiggington." I left as quick as I could.

When I looked back, she was standing at the door with another beer in her hand and she was still smiling.

****

I went back to the house, made myself some tea and forced myself to think things through. I could feel myself hating Mrs. Wiggington for stealing Charlene away from me and I could feel myself hating Charlene for wanting to go with her. But, then I knew if I ever had a little son and he went missing and then I found him a whole bunch of years later, I would want to bring him home to our little house on the hill, and let him see Big Dog, well, if Big Dog were alive, and give him biscuits fresh out of the oven and watch him breathe while he sleeps on our bed. And I'd guess I would want him coming home by hisself and not bring a whole bunch of people I didn't know with him. I could understand all that but I still wanted my Charlene. I didn't want to be alone again. Maybe I should get a new Big Dog.

A new Big Dog. A new Big Dog. That was a nice idea but still it seemed like just a dog wouldn't be enough for me any more. I wanted Charlene.

And my baby. I would be a good daddy. I would take good care of him. Play with him. Get him toys. Maybe make him a swing like they did Charlene. He would like that. Kids like swings. It was one of the first things Charlene mentioned when Mr. Green asked her what she remembered; the swing that hung from the big oak tree.
I suddenly had a bad feeling I couldn't identify.
The swing that hung from the old oak tree.
I went and looked under the bed for those papers I took to Charlene way back when I was trying to make her happy in the jail. She didn't seem all that interested in them and she would always give them back to me. I kept them in case I needed to bring something back for her again. I pulled out the stack and went through them one by one, looking at the pictures until I came to the one I didn't want to find.

****

I couldn't sleep that night. I just rocked back and forth on the bed until the sun came up. Then I went to town. I stopped in at the drug store for a few minutes. When I got to the courthouse, I found Pammy in the hallway and I nodded to her but walked away without even a good morning.
I saw Mr. Green talking with Mrs. Wiggington over by the trial room door. Mr. Green waved at me to come over but I looked away from both of them and kept walking until I found Mr. Dawson sipping his cup of coffee at the end of the hallway. Then I stood in front of him and muttered over and over, "The swing that hung from the old oak tree that Charlene loved so much" and he looked at me as though I were crazy and maybe I was. I held up the old newspaper in front of me. He stared at it for a minute and then I folded it up, put it in my pocket and turned and walked back down the hall. Mr Green was at the end of it and he had been watching me and Mr. Dawson.
"Billy Ray!" He tried to grab my arm, but I pulled away and ran out of the building. I walked home and slept all day while the trial went on.

I opened my eyes when it got dark. I looked around at the empty room and then I closed them again and went back to sleep. I didn't dream at all that night.

****

I woke up and the house seemed like a big empty box. The house was silent and I sat on the edge of my bed and wondered if I was even alive. I was still dressed from the day before and I walked to the door and picked my coat up off the floor where I had dropped it. I walked back down the road to the courthouse.

****

January 13 - Day Five
I don't know if that is exactly right because I didn't count yesterday. I really don't care anymore what day it is.
I went and sat down on my bench. Mr. Green turned and looked at me. Then Mr. Dawson turned and smiled at me. I had the urge to run out of the courthouse again but I stayed in my seat and the judge called the court to order.
Mr. Dawson started his day by calling Mrs. Wiggington to the stand. I must have jerked or made a sound or something because Mr. Green smiled over at me and mouthed, "Don't worry."
Charlene smiled for the first time since she had been in the courtroom. Mrs. Wiggington blew her a kiss and Charlene put her hand to her face and blushed.
Mr. Dawson welcomed Mrs. Wiggington to the stand and thanked her for her willingness to share with the court the reuniting of her family with her long lost daughter, Cheryl.
"It's my pleasure," Mr. Dawson.
"I know how hard this must be considering the reunion has come under such difficult circumstances."

Mrs. Wiggington disagreed. "Finding my daughter after all these years is welcome in any circumstance. I love Cheryl and no matter what she has done, I will always love Cheryl."

"I understand Mrs. Wiggington, I understand."

Mr. Dawson cleared his throat and rubbed his hands together. "Please tell the court the whole story of how Cheryl disappeared from your life and how she came back into it."

Mrs. Wiggington told the whole story and the female members of the jury wept loudly and Mr. Green looked happier with each tear they shed.

Then Mr. Dawson started clapping, very slowly, letting the court know what he thought of her testimony.

"That was most heartfelt, Mrs. Wiggington, and certainly everyone here in the court can sympathize with your plight. Too bad the defendant isn't really your daughter."

Mrs. Wiggington's mouth dropped open and she stared at Mr. Dawson. She tried to speak, but Mr. Dawson quickly cut her off with, "That's all for this witness, Your Honor."

The judge looked over at Mr. Green who was looking over at me and I had no place to look but at the worn spot on the floor in front of me.

"Mr. Green. Your witness?"

Mr. Green slowly shook his head. "No questions, your Honor, no questions."

"Call your next witness, Mr. Dawson."

"Will Mr. Wiggington please come to the stand?"

Some man I hadn't seen before in the courtroom walked to the front and sat down. I looked over at Mrs. Wiggington and I could see her glaring at him, so I guessed it was the husband she didn't live with any more. I didn't like the man the minute I laid eyes on him. It wasn't a matter of what he was going to say because I knew what he was going to say, but I hated him because he was the kind of person who deserved hating.

"She ain't my daughter."

"Can you repeat that, Mr. Wiggington?"

"She ain't my daughter. I don't know what my wife's been smoking, but that girl ain't my daughter."
Mr. Dawson tried to look puzzled.
"Why do you say she isn't your daughter? She says she is and your wife says she is?"
Mr. Wiggington snorted. "Yeah, well, then she's come back from the dead."
"Why would you think your daughter is dead?"
"Well, my wife left a piece of the story out, didn't she? The part about my daughter's coat being found in that pervert's trunk?"
A cry escaped from Mrs. Wiggington's mouth and she fled the courtroom.
"Go on, Mr. Wiggington."
He folded his arms over his big belly.
"Well, they found her coat and they asked my wife if it was our daughter's and she told them it wasn't. Then they came and asked me and I would have known that coat anywhere. There weren't two like it in the whole of Arkansas."
"My wife let the damn murderer of my daughter walk because she couldn't goddamn accept the fact that she was gone!"
Mr. Dawson swung around and bowed to Mr. Green.
"Your witness, Counselor."
Mr. Green got to his feet and faced Mr. Wiggington.
"Could you prove it was her coat?"
"What?"
"I repeat. Could you prove it was your daughter's coat?"
Mr. Wiggington's face grew red.
"I didn't have to prove it was her coat. It was her coat and if my wife had said it was, the police would have arrested the man."
"Did you have any pictures of your daughter wearing that coat?"
"Pictures? I don't know what pictures my wife took of my daughter. I saw her twice in the coat before I left and then I don't know what my wife did. She knew where I was even if she says she didn't and she didn't send me no pictures."

"Did you have a sales receipt for the coat?"
Mr. Wiggington looked annoyed. "My wife made her that coat, so why would we have any sales receipt?"
"Just answer the question, Mr. Wiggington. Did you have a sales receipt for the coat?"
"No!"
"Did you have a picture of the coat?"
He spoke through gritted teeth.
"No!"
"And so you had no proof, did you, Mr. Wiggington, that the coat in the suspect's car belonged to your daughter?"
"No, for Christ's sake, no!"
"Then what proof do you have that your daughter is dead, Mr. Wiggington, and that this woman sitting here is not your adopted daughter, since DNA isn't going to help prove she is?"
"None, you fucking prick, none."
The judge told him to watch his mouth or he'd get him for contempt of court.
Mr. Green did not seem the least disturbed by the outburst. He smiled and thanked Mr. Wiggington for his time. He then shot a glance over at Mr. Dawson who smiled back at him, also not the least bit disturbed by Mr. Wiggington's outburst.
The judge recessed for lunch.

****

Mr. Green cornered me in the lunchroom.
"What the hell is going on with you today, Billy Ray? Why are you so jumpy? Is there something you want to tell me?"
I couldn't speak. I don't know why I went to Mr. Dawson instead of Mr. Green. I felt like I had stepped in front of a train that I knew was coming because I didn't want to be confused any more.

I shook my head and avoided his gaze. He finally gave up trying to get me to look at him and walked away.

Charlene was called to the stand first thing in the afternoon. She didn't have to go up there but she did, against the advice of Mr. Green. She sat down quietly in the witness stand and the judge asked her if she understood she didn't have to take the stand and answer questions. It was her right not to testify in her own defense. She nodded.

"I need a verbal answer, Ms. Wiggington."

"Yes, sir, I understand."

The judge sighed and Mr. Green shook his head. "Go ahead, Mr. Dawson."

Mr. Dawson asked her name and she told him Cheryl Wiggington.

"And your middle name?"

Charlene seemed to stop and think a bit.

"I can't remember it."

Mr. Dawson walked back to his table and picked up the newspaper clipping I had seen at the hospital.

"Does this help?" He pointed to the caption under the picture of Charlene at six years old.

She smiled. "Oh, yes. Bettina. Funny name, don't you think?"

Mr. Dawson smiled back at her. "Yes, Cheryl, that is a strange name."

"You were a sweet little girl in that picture, Cheryl. Can you tell us a little about that girl and what you remember right before your family lost you?"

Charlene looked off into some void and started repeating what she had told Mr. Green and me in the little talking room that day. Actually, I could hear the words echoing in my head as though she had memorized each one of them.

She said, "I don't remember very much at all. I remember a little house. It was blue with white shutters. I remember a big ugly tree in the yard with a rope swing on it that I loved a lot. I remember the kitchen. It was yellow. I remember my mother. She had long blonde hair, and long

fingernails, and her teeth stuck out funny and they hurt sometimes when she kissed me. I had a little brother and sister."
Mr. Dawson asked, "And your father?"
She looked coldly over at Mr. Wiggington.
"I didn't have a father."
Mr. Dawson walked up to her and patted her hand.
"Thank you, Ms. Wiggington, that's all."
I could see Mr. Green's face from where I sat. He was totally confused and I almost laughed to see him feel like me. He was surely wondering what was the point of Mr. Dawson calling Charlene as a witness just to introduce exactly the point Mr. Green was planning to make. That Charlene suffered from that PTSD thing she got after she lost her family. Mr. Green wasn't going to question his luck. Maybe the prosecutor was losing his courtroom technique.
He walked up to Charlene.
"What do you remember after you were abducted?"
"Abducted?"
"Do you remember being abducted?"
Something odd passed over Mr. Green's face, like he forgot something and then remembered it.
He looked carefully at Charlene and said slowly, "You remember nothing at all, Ms. Wiggington, nothing at all?" He locked eyes with Charlene. She just stared for a bit and then she finally responded.
"I remember there was a man, a bad man...like a ghost that always was around. I, I...I don't remember who he was or what he did to me. I was very scared of him." Her voice trailed off and I wondered that this wasn't supposed to be the kidnapper who kept her and did terrible things to her, the man she was supposed to have confused with Mr. Doe.
Mr. Green laughed a bit sadly.
"You don't know who he was or what he did to you, but just the thought of him..." Mr. Green was letting the jury imagine her fear. "And you don't remember giving birth to any babies?"

Charlene shook her head. Mr. Green was pretty smart there. He made her look like she lost her memory right off.

"I don't remember leaving my family. I just remember that they used to be there and then they weren't."

"What is the next thing you remember after the time you described here in court?"

She hung her head. "Nothing until I was living on the streets in Bald Eagle."

Mr. Green presed her again. "You sure you don't remember giving birth to your babies? Your babies?

Charlene burst out crying. I was shocked. I never saw her just suddenly cry like that. She covered her face and she sobbed and I felt like I wanted to run up to the stand and stop the whole bunch of questions. Maybe what I had done was wrong. Maybe I was wrong about Charlene again. I just don't know what kind of wrong.

Mr. Green waited patiently until Charlene's sobbing finally slowed down. "Please answer the question, Cheryl. Don't you remember your babies?"

Charlene shook her head and through the tears still rolling down her face, she whispered, "No."

She put her head down in her arms on the witness stand and I felt like that Judas in the Bible. I watched Mr. Green help Charlene from the stand and I knew he had convinced the jury that she was suffering some sort of weird ailment that might just mean she was crazy when she killed Mr. Doe.

"I have one more witness to call to the stand, Your Honor." Mr. Dawson was speaking.

The judge looked up at the clock. "We are getting mighty long in the day, Counselor. Will you need much time with this witness?"

"No, sir. I only have one question."

"Go ahead, Mr. Dawson."

Mr. Dawson turned around. "Is Mrs. Wiggington back in the courtroom? Someone shouted out that she was in the hallway.

"Bailiff, could you gather up Mrs. Wiggington and bring her back in here?"

The bailiff went out and Mrs. Wiggington was found in short order and she sat back on the witness stand.

"Just one question, Mrs. Wiggington. What did you hang on the oak tree in your yard after your daughter went missing?"

Mrs. Wiggington swallowed hard. "I hung up a swing, sir. For my daughter so she would find her way home to it. She always wanted a swing."

I couldn't breathe. No one in the courtroom spoke.

Mr. Dawson turned to the court reporter.

"Would you please read back the part of the defendant's testimony where she told us of what she remembered in her childhood?"

The court reporter scanned backwards in her notes.

"Yes, Sir. Here it is."

"Please read it for the court and jury, Miss. Just the first four lines, please."

Ms. Wiggington said, "I don't remember very much at all. I remember a little house. It was blue with white shutters. I remember a big ugly tree in the yard with a rope swing on it that I loved a lot."

Mr. Dawson looked back at Mrs. Wiggington.

"When did you say you hung the swing on the oak tree?"

"One week after Cheryl disappeared."

"No more questions."

Mr. Green followed me out of the courtroom and punched me in the face. The police had to pull him away. I lay on the ground for a long time until I could see again. I didn't press charges.

IV

The case got thrown out because Mr. Dawson did a slick TV thing that you really aren't supposed to do in real life, hiding new evidence from the defense attorney and then making him look an ass in court. A new trial was scheduled for the beginning of March.

Mr. Green came by a couple of weeks later and apologized for breaking my nose. He handed me a bunch of twenty dollar bills.

"What's all this for?" I asked him.

"Look, I'm sorry I nailed you at the courtroom. It was unprofessional and not real nice of me. I know you ain't been able to do too much snow shoveling and you are out of money."

I took the money from him and put it under the butter dish. "Thanks. That's real nice of you."

I made some tea and some of my flat biscuits.

I asked him about Charlene.

"No, Billy Ray, she ain't asked about you since the trial."

I didn't know to be happy or sad. I didn't even know what to call her by. Cheryl, Charlene, or Jane Doe like Mr. Doe.

"Can I see the paper you found, Billy Ray?"

"Paper?"

"Yeah, the one you brought Charlene when she was in jail before she started remembering who she was."

I got up and pulled out the family Bible where I had put the paper between the Bible pages. I thought it was kind of funny to put it there because I don't know where the family Bible came from and it wasn't our family's name written in it anyhow but some other family named Griffith.

I slid the paper out and handed it over to Mr. Green.

He looked at the picture in the middle of the clipping. It was an ugly oak tree with a rope swing hanging off of it. Below the picture it said, "Family hangs swing and hopes for daughter's return."

Mr. Green read a little further and put the paper down on the table. He motioned for me to put it back. I slipped it back into the Bible and put the Bible back on the shelf.

"How did you know what it said, Billy Ray?"

"When I saw that picture, I had a bad feeling and I went to Mr. Snyder at the drug store and he read me the story."

"Why didn't you come to me instead of Mr. Dawson?"

I hung my head.

"I guess I was so upset or mad that I just didn't want to help Charlene any more and I figured you would just tell me to pretend I didn't see the picture."

Mr. Green actually laughed.

"Well, I guess you have learned how we lawyers work, Billy Ray. I sure would have told you to keep it to yourself."

Mr. Green rocked back in his chair and looked down his nose at me.

"You are finished with Charlene, aren't you?" he asked.

I had thought so before I ratted her out. But, then I saw her crying in the court and I was back to not knowing what to think or do."

"Why did she tell us she was Cheryl, Mr. Green?"

He shrugged. "I guess because it made a good story. She knew we were looking for a good story to defend her with."

"She really liked her new family, though. She was happiest I had ever seen her since she came to me."

"Billy Ray, you are the nicest man I have ever known. You still think something good about that girl no matter what she does, even after you got so hurt by what she did. Have you forgiven her already?"

I looked down at the table. "She isn't all bad, really, Mr. Green. She was good to me before the old man came."

"I know she was, Billy Ray, I know she was."

We sat for a while and didn't say nothing.

"I don't think I am really such a nice man," I said.

"Why do you say that, Billy Ray?"

"Well, I turned on Charlene."

"You were upset because you realized she lied to you."

I shook my head slightly.

"I don't know if that was my real reason. I think I might have thought if I told Mr. Dawson and he told the court, then the Wiggingtons wouldn't take Charlene away."

Mr. Green chuckled.

"That is a bit devious there, Billy Ray!"

My face felt hot.

"Maybe if I hadn't done that, you could have gotten Charlene off. Maybe now she is going to die because of me, because I didn't want her to leave me."

Mr. Green reached over and punched me lightly on my shoulder.

"Hey, don't get so down on yourself. Chances weren't that good I could win anyway."

I rubbed my palms over my eyes. Mr. Green had a way with words. I wasn't sure how his losing the trial would change the fact that I did what I did.

Mr. Green looked me in the eye and winked.

"I said you were a nice man, not a perfect one. Christ, compared to Charlene you're a bloody saint, so stop kicking yourself."

Yeah, Charlene or whoever she really was.

"So what do you think Mr. Dawson is going to say about Charlene this time round?

"He doesn't have to say too much any more. He has even more proof that Charlene is a psychopath and my PTSD story bussed out of town with Cheryl Wiggington's family. All I have is a whore who lied to you, lied to the police, lied to the court, and lied to a family grieving over the loss of their little girl." He rolled his eyes, "Oh, and killed a harmless old drifter. I don't think there is a jury between here and Alaska that is going to have much sympathy for Charlene."

I felt something catch in my throat.

I realized my anger at Charlene had gone away. I wasn't mad at her any more. Even though she was all those things Mr. Green said, when she had been my Charlene, she had been a good Charlene. It was the old man who had made her change into the bad Charlene. I realized I didn't care about anything she had done before she moved into my house or after she was taken from it.

"Charlene is all I got, Mr. Green, and if she don't come home, I don't know what I am going to do." I knew he would think I'm a fool.

He sighed. "She's a danger to society, Billy Ray."

He pushed back his chair and got up from the table.

I looked up at him. "Maybe she just needs some help from one of those psychiatrists and she'd be all right."

"I don't think any psychiatrist can help her if she is a psychopath, Billy Ray. I hear psychopaths don't change no matter what kind of help you give them. And I don't think I can prove Charlene's crazy. I've tried hard, but Charlene is her own worst enemy with all those games she plays."

I stared at my hands and remembered how Charlene's fingers would weave through mine right before she went to sleep with her head against my palm. She was bad or she was crazy but either way, it seemed it didn't matter. I was going to end up alone again.

"I'll let you know if I'm withdrawing from the case," Mr. Green said, suddenly sounding tired. "I'll let you know soon."

****

I didn't hear from Mr. Green until the middle of February. When he showed up, he practically broke my door down beating on it until I got out of bed and let him in.

"Jesus God!" he puffed, his cheeks beat red from the below freezing temperature outside. "What the hell are you doing sleeping at two in the afternoon?"

"I was just lying down. I guess I dozed off."

He pulled off his mittens and blew on his hands.

"Have I got some news for you!" he hooted and I wondered what could make him so excited.

"About Charlene?"

"No. Still don't know anything about Charlene."

I didn't think anything else much mattered.

"What then?"

"I got information on our John Doe!"

"You know who he is?"

Mr. Green waved my question off. "No, I don't know that."

"Okay, you don't know who Charlene is and you don't know who John Doe is."

The man really made me crazy and my nose still hurt from when he punched it.

"Sit, sit. All right. Let me tell you." He was so excited I didn't interrupt him any more.

"Looky here." He pushed a paper over at me with two pictures on it. I looked down and felt my blood go cold.

"It's him, isn't it?" he asked.

I nodded. I would never forget that man's eyes.

"Hah! Knew it! I got a positive ID from the Sheriff, the liquor store man, and that motel owner over in Bald Eagle. That drifter really was the same guy."

I looked at the two pictures, the one facing straight out and the one facing sideways. They were the pictures you get took when they arrest you. I got them took when they said I killed the old man.

I pointed to what should be his name under the pictures.

"John Doe, " Mr. Green told me.

"John Doe? Is that his real name?"

Mr. Green laughed. "No, but it would be funny if it was. No, they never did figure out who he was. They said they ran his prints but came back with nothing."

"So what was he arrested for?"

He leaned forward on his hands. "Rape, Billy Ray. Rape. Charges ended up dropped but only because the victim disappeared. She was a hooker like Charlene."

He looked like a rapist.

"Do you think he raped Charlene?"

Mr. Green shrugged. "Anything's possible. She could have been fighting him off over there at that Bald Eagle motel. He could have tried to rape her."

I remembered the day I went for the cigarettes and came home to Charlene crying in the corner; the day she stopped talking.

"Do you think," I said slowly, "that he could have raped her while I was at the store?"

"It's possible."

"Can you rape a whore?"

Mr. Green slapped me on the forehead.

"Of course you can rape a whore. Just because she is saying yes over here, doesn't mean she is saying yes over there. Chances are he ain't exactly having nicey-nicey sex with her either. He would be hurting her while he's doing it."

"Could she have sex with me the same day if she was raped earlier?"

Maybe I shouldn't have been asking those kinds of things. Mr. Green started stammering. "I really don't know, Billy Ray, I really don't know, I don't know."

I couldn't help but ask one more question.

"If she was raped, wouldn't it be okay if she killed him?"

Mr. Green smiled. "Well, it would sure be okay with me and I might be able to find a jury who would think the same thing." "

Mr. Green picked up his folder, put the pictures back in it, and walked to the front door.

"I'll see you in court, Billy Ray."

He stepped onto the porch and then he turned back around.

"Oh, and, Billy," he said, "If Charlene did have sex with you after she might have been raped by John Doe, you just keep that between you and me, understand?"

I nodded and Mr. Green left. This time I understood.

****

Spring came early to Whitfield Glen.

When I opened the front door in the morning, the sunshine lit up the entire house and you could feel it warm on your face if you stood there for a bit. I could see the buds starting to show on the trees and there were birds singing now. They broke the quiet which made me near crazy in the winter, especially with Charlene and Big Dog missing from the house. The trial has been postponed and postponed again. Mr. Green was trying to get as much time as possible to dig up dirt on John Doe so as to make the jury hate him enough to let Charlene go or at least get her a lighter sentence. He even went so far as to get a story put in a state paper about how a young pregnant girl who killed a suspected rapist was being charged with capital murder and what a shame that was. It was a good story and made me feel really sad reading it so I am guessing other people would feel bad for Charlene too.

"Billy Ray!"

I squinted into the sun that had broke over the stubby pines that stood in a row behind dead John Doe's burnt house and I could make out the figure of Mr. Green carrying something under his arm. He was moving fast toward me, his step bouncier than I had seen over these last months, and there he was, standing in front of me, holding out a mud-brown puppy.

He beamed.

"I got you a new Big Dog, Billy Ray!" Mr. Green laughed and then shrugged his shoulder a bit. "Well, a new small Big Dog."

The puppy looked at me and yelped.

"Hey then, put the poor dog down, Mr. Green! He don't like being all held up in the air like that!" I felt myself grinning from ear to ear. He did look like my old Big Dog had looked when he was that little. I got down on the ground with him and he started licking my face all over. He smelt like dog food so I guessed Mr. Green had just fed him before coming out here.

Mr. Green patted me on my shoulder. "He's your good luck charm, Billy Ray. He is going to be the start of good things for you and Charlene. We are gonna win this case and bring Charlene and your baby home."

I stood up.

"Thanks, Mr. Green. It was real nice of you to find me a new Big Dog."

Mr. Green shoved a big bag he was gripping in his left hand at me.

"Dog food. I'll bring you some more next time I get up here."

I carried the bag into the kitchen and New Big Dog started running from room to room, sniffing everything out. Mr. Green and I sat down at the kitchen table and just watched him going crazy. I wondered if he could smell old Big Dog.

After a bit, I turned to Mr. Green.

"Have you found out anything about John Doe yet?"

Mr. Green shook his head. "Not yet, but don't worry. We have time before next month to get something on him and even if we don't, that one arrest record for rape ought to help sway the jury. And, I found a couple of witnesses we can pull in who spent time with him in jail. They never knew his name to be anything but John Doe because he never told them otherwise and he never told them anything about himself. On the other hand, they will testify that he was always very angry, prone to violence if you got in his way, and he was suspected of shanking his cellmate while they were in the exercise yard."

I didn't know what shanking meant but it sounded like raping so I thought that would be good in court.

I nodded. "Okay."

Mr. Green patted my hand. "We have a good defense now. Don't worry about it." I looked up at him, straight in the eyes, and it seemed like he was telling the truth, not that I was too good a judge of that.

"How's Charlene?" I hadn't seen her for a few days because I had sprained my ankle stepping off the porch in a wrong way and it was too hard to walk all the way to town on it with it hurting so bad. My truck was still just sitting there because I spent too much time with Charlene, now that she was being sweet to me again, and I had not been working enough to pay for the new battery it turned out to need.

"She's good, Billy Ray, she's good. She seems much calmer now. I see she is starting to show a bit now, too."

I felt proud. I had made a baby and when I put my hand on Charlene's stomach I could feel it swelling up under my hand. I never was much good at making anything and it was a nice feeling knowing I had finally done something.

"Tell her I'll be down in a couple of days. My foot is almost better."

Mr. Green got up to go.

"All right. I've got some work to do."

I reached out and shook his hand.

"Thanks for New Big Dog. That was real nice of you."

Mr. Green nodded.

"I'll tell Charlene to expect you soon. Take care."

New Big Dog ran up beside me and we watched Mr. Green walked back down the path to his car. It would be the last time I saw him.

****

I didn't make it to the jail until Friday. I tried twice, once on Wednesday and once on Thursday, but my ankle still hurt me too much. By Friday, I thought I could make it and I found myself a big stick to help take the weight off of my foot if the going got too rough.

New Big Dog came with me. I tried to tell him to stay but he wouldn't take no for an answer and trotted along behind me. Maybe they would let me bring him into the jail so Charlene could see him. She will like him, I can tell. He might cheer her up and keep her from being mad at me for not showing up for almost a week.

It took me near two hours to reach the edge of town. I never walked so slow in my life and now that I was walking on pavement, my foot was really starting to hurt me. I limped along, putting more of my weight on the stick, yelling at New Big Dog to come back every time he raced off to check out a new sight.

I only passed a few people that afternoon as I neared the jail. I tried to say hello to each of them but they seemed not to hear me. Then when I came into the waiting area of the jail, a guard rushed toward me and immediately told me New Big Dog couldn't come in. He wasn't very nice about it. I didn't bring any leash with me and I hated to just leave him in the street. I told him to sit and stay and he slumped down against the building and looked at me with "don't leave me here" eyes. I gave him a pat but I didn't have a choice. "Just stay. I'll be back in a bit." I left my walking stick next to him so he'd know I'd return.

I went on inside but I didn't get more than a few feet when the Sheriff grabbed me by the arm and shoved me into a small office they have up front for talking to people who probably don't want to talk to them at the moment, but just want to see who they come to see. He pushed the chair away from the metal table and shoved me into it

Sheriff Hathaway didn't look any too pleasant.

"What are you doing here, Billy Ray?" He practically snarled at me, his bushy eyebrows coming close together like they were defending his eyes. I shook my head. I thought a policeman ought to be able to figure this one out. Maybe he was messing with me. The Sheriff's stare made me nervous. "I'm here to see Charlene, like always," I stuttered. "I know I haven't been here for a week but my foot got messed up." Maybe she told the Sheriff she didn't want to see me. Maybe she was mad at me for not finding a way down the hill. I kind of wondered why Mr. Green hadn't offered me a

ride but I guess he didn't want to have to make the round trip twice to get me back home once I was finished visiting Charlene.

"Is that right?"

Something seemed really wrong.

I shifted from one side of my chair to the other.

The Sheriff raised an eyebrow. "You want to see that woman, that murderer, that poor excuse for a human being?"

The small room was hot. The words of the sheriff burned into me. I wanted to get out of there, but he had shut the door and he was a cop so I just sat there, feeling his hatred for me. I didn't know why he suddenly hated me so much, so much more than the day he arrested me for killing the old man.

I attempted a diversion. "Is Mr. Green here today?"

The sheriff sniggered. "Yeah, right. At least he knows when to call it quits."

I felt a cold sweat break out on my face and neck.

"Quit?" I could hardly get the word out.

Sheriff Hathaway slammed both fists down on the table. "Quit! Yeah, you dumb ass, quit, like in sometimes even a defense attorney doesn't want to defend his client."

"He's gone?" I couldn't believe what I was hearing. Gone? Why? When? "What? Why didn't he tell me?"

The Sheriff stood up. "I don't know. Maybe he just doesn't like being lied to, Billy Ray. At least not by people he is trying to help."

He grabbed the door knob and, as if he had an afterthought, turned toward me. "By the way, we know who Charlene is, so you can stop pretending you don't."

The Sheriff flung open the door and strode out. The door knob clanged against the metal pole supporting the roof and came back and shut me in the room.

****

I was stifling to death in that 12-foot-square box. I felt weighed down to the chair, afraid to get up, terrified to open the door because I knew there was an explanation on the other side I didn't want to know. I wanted to run out, grab New Big Dog and go home, pretend I never met Charlene. I must have sat there for a long time, trying to decide which direction to walk when I came out of the room. Out of the corner of my eye I could see the light shifting on the wall and the room growing dimmer. I wondered how cold it would be if I had to walk home after dark, if visiting hours were over, if New Big Dog had given up on me and wandered off. I worried I might never see him again.

I became aware that someone had opened the door and was standing there looking at me. A big man, dark-skinned, the hair that he still had on his head trimmed close, blue trousers, white shirt overflowing the belt, a layer of body fat behind it. Neat tie.

The man sidled in the room and shut the door behind him. He plopped into the chair the sheriff had left empty, dropped his briefcase onto the table and offered his hand.

"Joe Stanley, public defender," he stated. "I'm taking over for Mr. Green."

The man looked worn, like he'd done this work for far too long and he should have retired ten years ago.

"You Charlene's lawyer now?" I asked suspiciously.

"Yeah." He breathed heavily.

"And?"

"And," he shrugged, "I will go to court, say a bunch of meaningless stuff, and the jury will come back with a conviction. That's the life of a public defender."

I stared at him.

He opened his mouth as though he were about to continue. Then he yawned.

"What about Charlene's defense?" I asked.

"You got one for me?" he shot back.

"Mr. Green said Charlene was raped by John Doe. He scared her."

Mr. Stanley drummed his fingers on the table, touching each dent he could find in a row.

He let his breath out slowly and looked at me. He seemed to be sizing me up. I hadn't had many people do that since I never spent much time with any until I ended up down at the court but I saw Mr. Green doing it to others. Then he would tell me something bad about them.

Then he asked me a question.

"Are you just stupid or are you in on this whole act?"

I didn't understand what he meant.

"What?"

"Are you just stupid or did you help Kristen kill the old man?"

"Kristen?" I couldn't understand this new lawyer. I wished Mr. Green hadn't run out on Charlene.

He groaned. "Kristen, Charlene, Kristen. Whatever you want to call her."

My eyes blurred. I couldn't breathe through my nose. I felt something dripping out of my nose and water running down my cheek.

Mr. Stanley's big hand reached out and grabbed my left shoulder.

"Don't you know why Mr. Green quit?"

I shook my head and rubbed my hand across my nose and then brought it under the table to my pants' leg.

The lawyer slumped back in his chair. "For Christ's sake, godallmighty. They told me you lived way up on some hill with this girl for two years and said you never even knew her name. I thought they were fooling me."

He leaned forward, opened the buckle on the briefcase in front of him and pulled out a newspaper.

He squinted at me. "You telling me you don't know why Mr. Green left and you haven't seen the newspaper either?"

I shook my head again.

"She never told you her name was Kristen? She never told you what happened over in Tennessee?"

My head felt like a big stone.

He shoved the paper in front of me. I looked down and I saw a picture of Charlene's face and some man's face and big writing that looked black and angry.

"Well? Well?" Mr. Stanley was watching my face.

I shook my head again.

He snorted. "You got nothing to say?" He had an incredulous look on his face.

"I can't read it," I said. "I don't read."

Mr. Stanley let out a slow whistle, reached forward and put his big palm flat down on the paper. He slowly turned it all the way around toward himself.

He started reading slowly, like I couldn't understand spoken words either. "Family murdered."

He paused.

"Family found murdered in their beds. Early this morning just after midnight, neighbors reported seeing a fire on the Stoddard property at the end of Collins Road where it meets County Road C. When firefighters arrived, the main house and a small shed adjacent to the driveway were fully ablaze. It took hours for the firemen to put out the fire. Five bodies were located in two bedrooms - the master bedroom and a bedroom at the end of the hall. A male and a female were found deceased in the king-size bed and three small children were found also deceased in the smaller room. Police Chief Morris Williams told reporters that the bodies were in such bad condition, identifying them would be difficult but neighbors confirmed Thomas and Mary Stoddard were at home that night and were taking care of their three grandchildren for their daughter, Kristen, who was out for the evening."

Mr. Stanley continued without looking up.

"Chief Williams has issued a warrant for the arrest of 17-year-old Kristen Stoddard," Mr. Stanley stopped a shook his head. "Your Kristen must have been quite an out-of-control teenager....pregnant at, what, age thirteen? Talk about the bad seed." He rolled his eyes. "Anyway, yeah, a

warrant for 17-year-old Kristen Stoddard, a white female, and a warrant for 58-year-old Rubin Covey, a black male. Williams warns that if any citizen sees these two, they should immediately call law enforcement and do not attempt to hold them in custody themselves. Williams states they are considered armed and extremely dangerous."

There was a buzzing in my ears that I wished would stop. I wanted Mr. Stanley to shut up and go away.

I pushed the paper away from me.

"Billy Ray," he was saying from what seemed a long distance away.

"Charlene and her old lover, Mr. Covey, shot her parents, poured gasoline over them and set them on fire. They locked the children in their room, gasoline splashed everywhere, and burned them up as the four-year-old and three-year-old tried desperately to escape. The baby died in the crib."

I was gonna throw up. I pushed away from the table and turned to the corner where I had seen a small metal trash bin. I heaved and heaved until my stomach hurt as bad as my head. Then, I slowly turned back toward the table. Mr. Stanley had put the newspaper away but now he was shoving a picture toward me. I didn't know why he needed to show me anything more.

I looked down and saw the face of the black guy that was in the newspaper. He wasn't smiling.

The lawyer tapped the photo with his index finger.

"Mr. Covey."

I nodded miserably.

Then he turned over the picture and pointed to some old writing on the back. It was faded and hard to read. But, even I, who couldn't read and could hardly keep my eyes clear, recognized my own name.

I look up questioningly at Mr. Stanley.

His gaze was steady. "We found this hidden away under a loose tile in Kristen's..." he nodded at me, "Charlene's... jail cell. She must have had it with her the day she came in after her arrest.

"You ever seen this photo before?"

I shook my head no.

"Never saw it at your house?"

"No."

"And you never met Kristen, Charlene, whatever, before she came to town?"

"No."

"And you don't know this Rubin Covey from Tennessee?"

"No."

Mr. Stanley pursed his lips.

"Then, why, Billy Ray, would she have a picture of Rubin Covey with your name scribbled on the back of it? Written, not by Kristen, because we checked that out, but by Rubin himself. Why would Rubin write your name down if he didn't even know you? And why would Kristen end up coming to you, Billy Ray? There has to be some logical answer, wouldn't you say?"

I finally raised my eyes to meet his.

"I don't know, Mr. Stanley. I don't know no Rubin Covey and I don't understand nothing except I don't believe the Charlene I knew would kill little children and her Mama and Papa. In two years of living with her, I don't know how I couldn't see she would be that kind of evil."

"Then again you didn't even know her name or that she was a whore or that she would kill a man either, did you, Billy Ray?"

I hung my head. I hadn't known any of that nor that she would lie to me over and over again.

"How come the police never caught her? And what about this Mr. Covey? Did they get him?"

Mr. Stanley pulled out a handkerchief and wiped at his forehead. "Damn hot in this room." He stuffed it back in his pants' pocket. "The police had an APB on them for a long time but no one ever saw the couple. Seems they must have separated at some point and Kristen ended up prostituting along a bunch of truck stops. She must have blended in with the other girls and no one ever figured out who she was. If the newspaper hadn't printed the story Mr. Green gave them about the poor pregnant woman who murdered her rapist, the Sheriff would never have gotten the tip that Charlene was really Kristen Stoddard."

He stopped talking and it got quiet in the room. It was dark outside and all the visitors had left for the day.

"Why would Charlene do such a thing?" I whispered.

Mr. Stanley took deep breath and let it out.

"Some things you just can't explain, Billy Ray, even if you wished you could. Maybe she wanted her freedom - got sick of them kids and her parents - or maybe she just likes killing people. Maybe she thought she was in love with this Mr. Covey and her kids and his wife kept them apart. I don't know." He had a look on his face like he had seen this all before and said the same words to somebody else who was sitting in the visiting room at a jail.

"So," I said slowly. "You aren't going to do nothing to defend Charlene?"

"Like I said before, no jury is going to have sympathy for her any more. It wouldn't matter how much work I put into this case, anyhow, because if she isn't convicted here, she will just be sent back to Tennessee and they got the death penalty there as well." He grunted. "Besides," he reached back in his briefcase and pulled out a shiny 8 by 11 photo. He looked at it and then carefully placed it in front of me.

I closed my eyes before I could see what it was.

"Open your eyes, Billy Ray," Mr. Stanley commanded.

I knew I was going to see something bad.

"Open them."

I slowly lifted my eyelids up a little and I felt my stomach heave again. It was a picture of the old man, what was left of the old man, charred, with his skeleton face and his empty eye sockets and grinning fake teeth, two sets of white and gray squares, still in their perfect rows except for the one chipped one under where his right cheek would have been. I felt the room reel. I had to look away.

"Not a pretty sight is it," Mr. Stanley said in a somewhat mocking tone. "Can you imagine how the jury will feel when they see what Charlene did to that poor old man, cooking him better than a well-done steak? I guess she had lots of practice charring her family to death."

The chair screeched against the floor as Mr. Stanley got up to leave. He picked up the big photo and slid it back into his briefcase. He started to reach for the small photo on the table, but for some reason I snatched it to myself before he could touch it.

"I want to keep this."

Mr. Stanley cocked his head to one side and looked at me kind of funny. He shrugged. "What the hell. Doesn't matter to me. No one ever told me it was evidence."

"Can I have the newspaper story too?"

The lawyer reached into his briefcase, pulled it out, and tossed it across the table to me."

"Knock yourself out."

Then he spoke once more before he opened the door.

"Take my advice, Billy Ray. Just let her go. She's poison. Go home."

I heard the door slam and I sat and stared at the pictures in front of me. I couldn't deny that this Kristen was Charlene and that Charlene was Kristen. I picked up the picture and brought it closer to my eyes. The man, this Mr. Covey, seemed somewhat familiar. I couldn't figure out why because I never been in Tennessee and I never heard of him.

I got up slowly and walked through the door Mr. Stanley had left open and went up to the reception desk. I knew the officer there pretty well by now.

"What can I do for you, Billy Ray?" he asked over his shoulder as he moved some piles of paper around on his desk.

"I need to see Charlene. I won't be but a minute. Please."

Ed looked up and signaled me over to the door which opened into the hall leading to Charlene's cell. I limped behind him until we got to the last one in the row. Charlene was curled up on her cot facing the wall.

"You got a visitor, Charlene," he called out and he let me in and disappeared back down the hall.
I went over to the cot and sat down on the edge and touched Charlene's arm. She tensed up her shoulders and didn't move or turn over towards me.
"I heard about everything, Charlene," I told her, my voice trembling. "I heard everything. Charlene, I need to hear the truth. From you. The truth. Only the truth."
She didn't answer or make a sound.
"Did you kill your family, Charlene? Your kids?" I almost choked on the words.
I felt her move just slightly. Then she rolled over and looked up at me with those clear blue eyes.
I held her gaze. "Only the truth, Charlene, only the truth."
She looked at me a long time.
"I love you."
And then she turned back toward the wall.

****

I stood by the door to the jail with Ed, staring blindly out at the street. What now? Do I go home and pretend Charlene never happened? How could she just kill her little children, why would she kill her little children? Was she that evil, as bad as everyone keeps telling me? I had questions that no one could seem to answer, that Charlene refused to answer. Maybe I would have to go find the truth myself, even if it was a bad truth, just so I could know, so I could stop believing Charlene loved me, so I could stop loving her.
I turned to Ed.
"Could you lend me $20, Ed?" I asked him.
Ed looked a bit taken aback. "Twenty bucks? What for?"
I couldn't quite look him in the eye.
"I gotta go to Charlene's town."

Ed groaned and ran his big hand through his shaggy brown hair.
"Billy Ray! Are you a masochist or something?"
I didn't know what masochist was, but I figured I was probably it.
"Geez Louise, give it up already. She's not worth it."
I shuffled my feet, kicking my left shoe against the wall, trying to knock off
a piece of mud stuck to it, then felt guilty for dirtying the place.
Ed was reaching for his wallet.
"Here. Take it." He pushed a green bill toward me.
I reached out and took it from his hand and shoved it down in my back
pocket
Ed looked at me solemnly.
"You even know where to go?"
I shook my head.
Ed sighed.
"Hold on." He walked across the room and disappeared into an office.
When he came back, he handed me a piece of lined paper, folded up.
I opened it up and looked at the two words scrawled across the paper.
Something and something.
I looked up at him.
"Oh, shit. I forgot. Sorry." He pointed to each word. "Jenkins. Tennessee."
Then he grabbed me by the shoulders and turned me toward the east.
"Route 40, cross the Mississippi, and about one hundred fifty miles more."
"Okay." I turned and stuck out my hand.
He gave me a strong shake, slapped me on the back, shook his head and
sighed again.
"Good luck to you, Billy Ray. I don't know what the point is but I hope
you get what ever you need from going there."
"Thanks, Ed. I'll get you your money back as soon as I can."
"It's okay. Go on."
He opened the door for me and I stepped out onto the dark street. I turned
to the spot where I left New Big Dog but there was just empty space there.
My walking stick was gone, too.

I scanned the street to the left and then the right and back to the left again.

"New Big Dog!" I yelled."New Big Dog?"

I heard the door click behind me.

The street was silent.

"New Big Dog! Where are you?" I started running, as best I could with my messed up foot, looking down between the buildings, each one, until I got to the end of the street. Nothing. Nothing.

I turned around and now my foot was really hurting and I was only half-running back down the other way.

"New Big Dog!" My voice bounced off the walls of the jail and then sounded quieter each time I yelled out as the buildings got farther apart and I arrived where it dead-ended at the railroad tracks. I squinted as I tried to see as far down the tracks as I could, searching for any shape that moved. All I saw was the shiny rails disappearing into the hills.

"New Big Dog?" My voice didn't have much in it any more. I knew he had gone away, given up on me when I didn't come out of the jail for so long.

I felt empty. I started walking slowly toward the highway, hoping that I would see him somewhere before I left town. I felt like a dog myself, failing Charlene, leaving New Big Dog. I was glad I was alone and no one could see me. I wasn't worth nothing. I had nobody. I had no friend. I didn't even know why I was going to Tennessee except something in my head told me I had to go.

****

V

It took me until near midnight before I got a ride. I guess I wouldn't have wanted to pick me up neither, looking like some bum in the dark, maybe someone dangerous. But, then Mickey stopped.
"You needing a lift?" He was in a big rig, a shiny red one, and he was so high up he seemed like he was in the second story of a building looking down from a window.
He pushed the door open and signaled me up. I have short legs and it was a big climb. I had to grab hold of his hand and let him pull me up. I settled down on a big red seat with a rip in it held closed by gray duct tape. It scratched my hand. I hauled the door closed behind me.
Mickey was a big, big man. Flaming red hair to match the truck and a big beard that looked like I could use it to scour my pots. Friendly looking, though.
The truck roared off onto the road and I felt like I was watching a picture show beneath me.
He started laughing at me looking down.
He had a loud voice.
"Never been in a rig like this, buddy?"
"No, never." I grinned because, in spite of my situation, it was pretty cool to be riding in the truck.
"I'm Mickey. You?"
"Billy Ray."
"Billy Ray! So, where you heading, Billy Ray?" He reached with his right hand into his shirt pocket and pulled out a box of Marlboro Reds. He must really like the color red. He shook the pack. grabbed a cigarette with his teeth, and pulled it out. He shoved them at me and I pulled one out of the box.
He put the pack back into his pocket and grabbed a lighter off the seat. He lit his and then handed me the lighter to light mine.

He inhaled and exhaled. I did the same; the cigarette calmed me a bit.
"I'm going to Jenkins in Tennessee," I told him.
"Jenkins?"
"Yeah." I looked at him hopefully. "You going anywhere near there?"
He grinned. "I'll be going by there, so you're in luck."
I breathed a sigh of relief.
"Family?"
I didn't know quite what to say. "Sort of."
"You ever been there?"
"No."
"Someone expecting you?"
"No."
Mickey honked his horn as a white car swung in front of him. "Asshole," he muttered.
He looked over at me. "You just gonna show up and surprise 'em?"
I didn't say anything.
He eyed me, suspiciously, looking at my shirt and pants and shoes.
"You not running from anything, are you?"
"No.
"You didn't just get released from jail?"
I wondered how he knew I was at the jailhouse.
"No, I wasn't in jail. I was just visiting someone."
"You got any drugs on you?"
I didn't know if he was getting scared of me or was hoping I would have some.
I shook my head violently. "I don't do no drugs."
Mickey looked relieved.
"So what the hell are you doing on the road at night going to a town you don't have nobody expecting you?"
I guessed I had to tell him the story of Charlene even if it did make me look like an idiot.

Mickey actually enjoyed my telling about what happened to me and Charlene and about my two Big Dogs. I guess I was entertaining and he could use something to keep his mind working and awake while driving in the dark.

"Woo hoo!" Mickey's booming voice took up the whole cab of the truck. "That is one heck of a tale if you are telling the truth! Dang! Crazy stuff!" He was steering the truck off the road into one of them all-night truck stop places with gas and a restaurant. I was feeling pretty hungry not having eaten all day.

Jumping down from the truck was easier than getting up into it. I could see trucks all lined up in a row, one color after the other. I wondered if I had known about driving one that I couldn't have gotten myself a job like that. But, I had never thought of going out of town. I looked up at the restaurant sign. It glowed and one part of it blinked. Downtown Truck Stop. Open. Open. Open. Open. I liked watching it flash. I wondered why it was called Downtown when we were in the middle of the highway.

"You don't get around much, do you?" Mickey said, grabbing me by the arm and hauling me toward the diner door.

It smelled real good. And it was busy. Lots of big guys like Mickey. Made me wonder if all truckers came in extra large. There were even some lady truckers sitting at the counter. All of them were talking and laughing and eating big plates of food.

"Hey, guys!" Mickey was slapping this one and that one on the back. "This here is Billy Ray. He's keeping me company tonight."

"Hey, Billy Ray!" The blonde truck lady gave me a smile and she moved over a seat so Mickey and I could have two seats together.

"Nice to meet you, Billy Ray." All the truckers were being real friendly to me.

The waitress put a menu in front of me. I ignored it and ran my eyes over the plates on the counter in front of the truckers. I picked out one that looked like it had good food on it. "I'll have that," I told her. I hoped it wasn't an expensive one because I didn't have much money to make it to Jenkins and back.

I had meatloaf and mashed potatoes and cornbread. I must have seemed real hungry because the waitress came back and gave me an extra couple of cornbreads. I wished I could come here again. I hadn't had such good food since Charlene...well, since Charlene.

"Hey, Billy Ray!" I looked over at Mickey, my mouth full of lima beans. He slapped the back of his hand on my jacket. "You got a picture of your girl? Maybe these guys might have run into her...." Mickey suddenly realized what he was saying. "Yeah, well," he cocked his head toward me and rubbed his bearded chin, "Maybe not."

I reached into my jacket and pulled out the newspaper picture of Charlene and that man, Rubin Covey. I carefully folded down the big letters above the pictures so that the truckers wouldn't see what Charlene had done. I held up the paper so they could all see it. I needed to find out what I needed to find out and it didn't matter so much to me what they thought of her or me.

There was a few seconds of silence while they were looking over at the picture, then one of them cleared his throat and said, "Yeah, I run into her."

I looked at the man. He was an older trucker and he seemed a bit embarrassed.

He looked quickly at me and said, "She's trouble. She ripped me off." "How did she do that?" I asked.

He looked defensive and annoyed at the same time.

"She just did," he said abruptly and got busy ripping open sugar packets and dumping them in his coffee.

"I saw her, too," another trucker offered, this one a bit younger and softer looking.

He looked a bit sheepish. "She, well, you know, she was 'visiting' at one of the other truck stops and I spent a bit of time with her." His eyes looked up and to the left. "I can't remember what she called herself, but she was nice enough to me."

"Was she alone?" I asked.

"Alone?" The trucker was trying to bring back his memory of her. "No, no, she was with some guy."

"Black guy?"

"Nah, white guy, older." He nodded his head up and down. "Yeah, I remember that guy. He lurked around and I wasn't sure about him. He gave me the willies."

I asked again, showing him the two pictures and pointing to the one of Covey on the right. "You sure it wasn't him?"

"Nope. White guy. "

The older trucker piped in. "Yeah, white guy, older than her, with a bit of a beard. I would say he was pimping her."

I put the newspaper back into my jacket. The counter got real quiet. Mickey leaned over my plate and handed the waitress a small stack of dollar bills. He glanced over at me. "I got this one." Then he signaled for me to get up.

We walked out the door and over to the truck.

"Hold up!"

The blonde lady trucker had followed us out.

She was a little thing. I wondered how she handled a big truck.

"Look here," she said and got in front of me. "I know this ain't none of my business and I'm not sure what you are wanting with that girl, so maybe I should be keeping my nose out before I cause someone trouble...," She looked like she was going to change her mind and not tell me whatever she had to say. But, then she continued. "There was something wrong with that girl," she said. "I have met a lot of girls who work the truck stops. Sometimes they like to talk with another female just to have some girl chatter, so I tried to be friendly with that one." She paused. "She....she was different than the others."

I started to feel good and I must have looked like I was getting a bit happy because then the trucker lady blurted out, "I don't mean different in a good way. I mean different in something was not screwed on right in that girl's head. When she looked at me, she seemed to have only two emotions that went back and forth; she was either completely cold...no, not cold...just nonexistent.. blank... totally blank....or.." her voice trailed off. "Or what?" asked Mickey.

"Or she seemed like she hated the whole world, not just the creep she was with, but all the men, the other ladies, the waitresses, me...everyone. I felt like if she got hold of a sharp knife, she would start slashing anyone within arm's length."

The lady trucker looked directly at me.

"Don't play with fire. I would stay far away from that girl if I were you." She turned and walked back toward the diner. Mickey and I got in the truck and pulled back onto the dark highway. Neither one of us spoke for the next hour.

The trucker lady's words kept going through my head. Don't play with fire. Don't play with fire. Yeah. Don't play with fire.

****

Mickey took me all the way to Jenkins like he said he would. I was sorry to see him go because he was a real nice fellow. I would have liked to have a friend like him. But he had a job to do, so I was all by myself again. My foot was feeling better so at least I could walk normal which I figured would be good when I got to meeting people in town. The center of Jenkins wasn't but a mile off the main road so I was right in the middle of it in no time. It was a pretty place, nicer than Whitfield Glen. It had a long row of colorful painted stores on Main Street and there was a sparking white church with a welcome sign that said "Come on in! God's Home is Your Home Too!" Of course, it was also four in the morning, so I was the only one on the street.

Except for the police officer who was now standing in front of me.

*He didn't smile and give me a welcome to town like the church.
"What are you doing here?" His eyebrows came close together in a clench
of disapproval. He had a nice face, a light brown color, and his hair was
wavy even though it was cut short. I guessed Charlene's and my baby
would grow up to look like him. My stomach tumbled and I wondered if
my baby would grow up in somebody else's family and I would never see
him.
I tried to think of a good answer.
"I'm looking for someone," I mumbled. It was the truth even if I didn't
know who that someone was yet.
"Who?"
He had to ask me that.
I searched my brain for an answer. I didn't find one.
"I don't know."
The officer's hand moved slightly toward the gun on his right side.
"Let me see some identification."
"I don't have none." I never had a reason for any ID before. I guess I
should have a license to drive the truck but no one ever bothered me about
it because I only went up and down the one road.
"Turn around!" He voice became sterner. "Put your hands on that wall in
front of you."
I did what he told me to do.
I felt his hands going in and out of my jacket pockets, and up my chest,
around my sides and across my back. Then he ran his palms up and down
my pants legs, right then left, which made me real nervous.
"Turn around."
He was holding my twenty-dollar bill, the newspaper article, and the
photo.
He waved the bill at me.
"This all you got?"
"Yes."
"What did you say your name was?"*

I didn't remember him asking before or me telling him.

"Billy Ray Hutchins."

His eyes narrowed. "Where are you from, Mr. Hutchins?"

I told him, "Whitfield Glen, over in Arkansas."

He gave me my twenty back.

We were under a streetlamp and he unfolded the newspaper and tilted it so the light would hit it.

He was looking hard at the pictures, taking his time reading it. He looked at the photo and held it next to the picture in the paper that was on the right of Charlene's. Then he flipped the photo over. His eyebrows went up a little. He looked back at me.

"Billy Ray Hutchins, huh?"

I wished now I'd left the photo on the table for Mr. Stanley to put back in his briefcase.

"Yeah."

The police officer moved in a little closer to me and my hands felt sweaty.

"You looking for Rubin Covey?"

"No!" I blurted out. I knew Covey was bad and I didn't want him thinking I had something to do with the things he had done.

"You looking for Kristen then?"

"No, no." I shook my head. I felt sweat come down from my hair even though it wasn't a bit hot at that time of the morning.

He was staring at me again and I looked away from his eyes. He made me feel like I had done something wrong when all I did was walk down the street.

He waved the newspaper and photo at me and then slapped them against his left palm. Then, he said "Well, I have got to get some work done."

I thought that was it then and I reached for the paper and picture.

He pulled them out of my reach.

"I'm not finished with you yet. You can come on down to the station with me and sit with me until you remember who you came here looking for."

He took my right arm with his left hand and started marching me down the street. We walked that way, me a little ahead of him, his hand grabbing just above my elbow, the whole two blocks until we reached the police station.

****

"Sit!" he commanded and I slumped into the chair opposite his big metal desk. He gave me that look again and I straightened myself up even though I was tired now and I wanted to sleep.
He sat down and started looking at some police reports, at least I guessed that's what they were since we were in a police station and the papers looked important.
"Anytime you want to let me in on your little mission...," he commented as he made some notes on a pad of paper.
I suddenly realized who the first person was I came to see.
"I'm here to see you."
The officer's looked up quickly and then sat back in his chair. A slight smile played on his face.
"Me? You came to see me?"
"Yes, sir."
"And why would that be?" He thought I was trying to trick him.
"Because you can tell me about Charlene...I mean, Kristen." Her real name felt like sawdust in my mouth. "And about Mr. Covey."
The officer leaned forward. I could see he had his name under his silver badge and I wished I could read it so I could be polite and use his name. Suddenly his face lit up. "Wait a minute! Are you that dumb shit Kristen shacked up with over in Whitfeld Glen and has wrapped around her evil little finger?"
I felt my face get hot.
He started laughing. He shook a finger at me. "You're the baby daddy!"
He rubbed his hands over his face and looked at me more seriously.

"What the hell are you doing here? What do you want me to tell you or show you? Do you want to see the graves of those babies over at the Bethlehem graveyard? You want to see the burnt ground where the house used to be? You want me to tell you what I saw that night when I went into the house after they got the fire put out?" His voice was becoming loud and angry. I looked down at my lap.

"Let me tell you something, Hutchins. Just because I'm cop doesn't mean I don't feel things. I got kids of my own, three babies just about the same age Kristen's children were when they got torched. Torched! Not even dead! Yeah, Covey and Kristen shot her parents, but the babies, they just shut them in the room and let them burn to death alive." I heard his voice waver. He cleared his throat. When I looked up at him, he had tears in his eyes. "I never saw anything so awful in my life, Hutchins." He looked up and blinked. He pressed his lips together and cleared his throat again. He looked at me coldly. "That's your little girlfriend, Hutchins. If she hadn't done in that old man, you might have come home one day and found your own house on fire and your own baby barbequed." He shrugged. "Or, maybe you are just like Covey, wherever the hell he is. Maybe Kristen has a type." He leaned forward a little. "Maybe you helped Kristen kill that neighbor of yours. Maybe you were hiding Covey up there in your little house up there on the mountain, Maybe the old man figured out what you three were up to."

I felt like I was in a someone else's dream. The policeman was spinning a story that seemed like it could be real if only it didn't have me in it. He was flipping the photo over again.

"This here is your name on the back of Covey's photo." He stopped and waited for answer the same as Mr. Stanley had done. I didn't have any better answer now and it wouldn't have mattered because I knew the dream was going to go on and I was going to find out how my name ended up there.

"So, Kristen had Covey's photo with your name on it. So they go looking for you, friend of Mr. Rubin Covey, and find a nice little hideaway in

Arkansas while we go nuts searching every cave and gulley in Tennessee trying to find them."

He looked at me again.

"Did you and Covey have a falling out? Was it over Kristen?" He wobbled his head back and forth like he was trying to tumble all the answers into place.

I just sat there with my mouth open.

He slammed his fist on the table. "Nothing to say?" He made a kissing noise with his teeth. "Do you know how long you will go to prison if you helped those two escape the law? Now, you better start telling me about your relationship with the two of them and where Covey is. I want to bring that bastard back to Jenkins and see him in the chair."

I knew he didn't mean the kind of chair I was sitting in but the one with electricity. I gripped the arms of my seat and shifted uncomfortably from my right leg to my left. My butt felt numb.

"I don't know nothing about Mr. Covey," I said, trying to get out of the bad dream the police officer had stuck me in. "I just know Charlene..Kristen...she was alone when she came to Whitfield Glen."

"With your name in her hand," he pointed out again.

"I don't know Mr. Covey," I insisted again.

He sighed and drummed his fingers on the desk.

"So, if I remember my demographics," he said and then he looked at me, "and that means how many of what kind of people are in a particular place, Mr. Hutchins - Whitfield Glen has only one black man and that would be you."

He looked smugly at me.

"And now, Kristin, a white girl from a town of five hundred, runs off with a black man who, until last year, just happened to be only one of five black men here in Jenkins. She coincidentally stumbles upon Whitfield Glen and goes straight to your home, a black man with his name on the back of another black man's picture. But, you don't know Mr. Covey."

I shook my head again.

"You know I can lock you up for vagrancy since you don't have any identification, no one to stay with...," he snickered and then paused for effect, "....since you don't know the Coveys, and you don't have enough money for even one night at a motel."

"By the way, you can call me Chief Williams. Chief Morris Williams." So I was talking to the police chief of the town. He made me nervous and I didn't want to be put in a cell.

Suddenly he smacked his hand down on the table and nearly knocked his police reports off.

"I know what I can do for you! I'll take you out to see the Coveys myself! I want to see if they are going to be excited to lay eyes upon Billy Ray Hutchins or not." He jumped up out of his chair and walked over to a coffee machine and started pouring the dark grounds into the cone-shaped filter. "No, I don't know what connection you've got to Rubin Covey but I am damned sure going to find out or you're going to wind up a permanent guest in our town, at least for the next 364 days." He started up the coffee machine, turned around and grinned at me.

I didn't like his attitude but at least I was going to start getting some answers. I was also getting a free cup of coffee, and I didn't have to pay a taxi to take me out to see those Coveys.

****

It wasn't that there were no black people around Jenkins, it was just that they mostly lived in the next town over, in Mitchelleville. Those Coveys and a couple other black families spilled over the line into the town where folks claimed their ancestors came from Germany which is why they were all big, stocky people, even the girls. Chief Morris Williams says he was the result of a romance between a neighbor girl and boy whose backyard gardens were on either side of the boundary line. He laughed and told me things were changing across the state and those lines between folks were disappearing, and soon things would change, even in Whitfield Glen way up there in the mountains.

We pulled up to the Covey house at 9:30 am. Chief Williams thought that would be an acceptable time to knock on a person's door. While we walked up onto the small gray porch extending from the front door, he warned me I was to just stand there and say nothing, let him do the talking. I guess he thought I might give the Coveys a coded word or something that would tip them off that they weren't supposed to know who I am.

Chief Williams knocked three times on the window pane because they didn't have a knocker or a bell. Then he rapped a few more times when no one came to the door. After another half a minute, we heard someone saying to hold on and a woman unbolted the slide lock and pulled the door back.

"Chief?" I guess she knew him but she didn't look overjoyed to see him. He beamed at her. "Hi, Mrs. Covey. Look who I brought to see you!" He put his arm around my shoulders and squared me in front of the woman. She looked at me but she didn't seem very impressed.

"Who?" she asked Chief Williams.

I bust out laughing and he cuffed me on the back of the head.

"Billy Ray Hutchins," he growled at her.

Mrs. Covey crossed her arms, putting her fists under her elbows. She was a woman who was probably in her middle fifties, with a few dozen more pounds than when she was young girl. She was tough. She meant business, and you didn't mess with her. She reminded me of my Aunty what I could remember of her.

"So? What am I supposed to want with him? Who is he?"

Chief Williams pulled out the photo and showed her my name on the back of it.

"Uh-huh...and?"

He turned the picture over and Mrs. Covey's expression froze on her face. She didn't take long to speak. She was angry.

"What kind of game are you playing, Chief?" You could have cut potatoes with her voice it was so sharp. "I don't know who the hell this man is you

have brought to my doorstep and I have told you time and time again I have no idea where my husband is at."

The Chief look rather chastised like his own mother had put him in his place. He actually apologized.

"I'm sorry, Mrs. Covey, I know you're telling me the truth. I just thought you would know this man and I could figure out what the connection is between him and your husband."

Mrs. Covey looked tired, tired of going through the same conversation over and over again. I knew just how she felt. Maybe she was caught up in Chief William's dream as well.

"I don't know him, all right?"

"Yeah, yeah. All right."

Chief Williams turned like we were going to leave but then he put his hand up on the doorframe and slumped against the wood.

"Can I ask you a favor, Mrs. Covey?"

"What kind of favor?" Mrs. Covey didn't like the sound of that question.

He straightened up, stepped back, and pushed me forward.

"Talk to this fool. He's in love with that girl your husband ran off with."

Her eyes snapped over to me and locked onto my face.

"Why the hell should I talk to him?"

The Chief actually spoke softly and kindly about me.

"I think he's a nice guy, Mrs. Covey, and he could use a little straight talk from someone with sense."

I knew the Chief was fooling her; he wanted us to talk to see if I would give up some information to Mrs. Covey that he could circle around and come get from her later. If she was honest like he said she was, she would tell him the truth even if it meant turning her husband in to the police and him ending up in that chair.

Mrs. Covey fell for it. Her face softened and her arms unfolded.

"Come in, Mr. Hutchins." And she pushed the storm door open so I could come through.

Chief Williams gave a nod.

"I'll wait out in the car. Take your time."
Mrs. Covey closed the door behind me and ushered me into her living room which was as blue and velvety as the inside of one of those jewelry boxes I had opened once when I was in the drug store.
"Sit!" she ordered, but much more sweetly than Chief Williams had in his office.
I sat in a blue chair and it felt really soft under me. I couldn't help but stroke the cushion just a little because it felt so good.
Mrs. Covey sat down opposite me on her couch.
She pushed her glasses slightly back up her nose.
"Are you really in love with that girl?"
I swallowed. "I think so."
"You think so? You don't know so?"
"Well, I loved her for three years but now Charlene...uh, Kristen...I call her Charlene... has me so confused...," my voice failed me.
"So have you got her hidden somewhere? Is that why the Chief has you here? Did you tell him where she is?"
I guessed she hadn't heard the news about Charlene.
"No, Ma'am. I mean, I didn't have to. Charlene is ready in jail."
Mrs. Covey breathed out heavily.
"So, they finally caught up with her."
"No, Ma'am," I tried to explain. "They didn't know she was living with me in Arkansas until she got arrested and someone recognized her picture and called Sheriff Hathaway and then he called Chief Williams I guess."
"She got arrested for what?"
"She...she...killed someone."
"Again?" The word ended in a high pitch. "And who did she do in this time around?" asked Mrs. Covey, her voice now sounding flat and sarcastic.
"An old man who lived across the road," I told her.
"Did she burn him up? Shoot him and then burn him up?"
"Yeah."

"Dear God!"

She got up and walked over in front of me.

"And you're still her man?"

I guessed I was.

She slapped me on the side of my head and my left ear started ringing.

She had a strong hand.

"What the hell is wrong with you, Mr. Hutchins? You take up with a woman who has murdered five people... wait, no...now, six people? What is wrong with you men? What is so special about this girl," she stopped, then added, "who ain't really nothing to look at? What is so amazing about this tramp that my husband had to get all caught up with her and her schemes and now you're hooked up in the same thing? Is she that good in bed? You all make me sick." She was huffing, blowing her cheeks in and out, clearly exasperated that Charlene had stolen her husband.

She turned to me angrily.

"And it isn't only about my husband leaving me. I could live with that. But to know he helped that girl kill those innocent babies...I wish I had never met the man. I curse the ground he walks on. To think...," tears welled up in Mrs. Covey's eyes and started down her cheeks, "I always believed him to be a good man. I thought he loved me, that he was a Christian the way he always read his Bible and talked to me of what Jesus required of us and how he wanted to please his God...."

She sniffed and pulled a Kleenex from her under her sweater.

"He used to tell me to feel sorry for Kristen, that she was really a sweet girl with low self-esteem who just let boys take advantage of her. Then one night, I drove into town late....well, Rubin was at work at the hospital over in Pitts...he was on the night shift working as an orderly...and I drove into town to gets some corn chips and soda, just felt like some corn chips and soda." She laughed a little sadly. "I can't stand corn chips any more."

"What happened then?" I asked.

She laughed halfheartedly again. "The damn convenience store was right next to that cheap motel; it costs so little that men don't mind paying the whole night rate for just an hour of fun. Well, I came out of the store with my bag of chips and my soda and got in my car. I was tearing into the chip bag and enjoying myself when I look across the parking lot and there they were...Kristen and my husband....all cuddly, his arm around her - a married man with an underage girl at that, still a child in my opinion, even if she acted like she was all grown up and was Satan's Seed - unlocking the motel room door. Number 21. I hate that number, too."
She shook her head.
"Anyway, they went in and closed the door. I remember looking at the car they were in and I had no idea whose it was. Kristen didn't have a car and I was sitting in our car. Rubin had ridden his bicycle to work."
She was silent for about a minute and I wondered if she was sitting in that lot again in her mind.
"An hour went by and out they came. They got into the unknown car and drove off. Then I drove home. When I got there, I thought I should have followed them but I was in such shock at the time, I just wanted to go home and sleep."
I felt really bad for Mrs. Covey. And I couldn't stand to think of Charlene with her husband.
"Did you talk to him when he came home?" I asked her.
She smiled thinly. "I never spoke with him again. I never heard him come home...he obviously did because when I got up in the morning and I went downstairs, I found a note that said he had to help a 'friend' move. I hadn't heard about any friend who was doing a major relocation. The whole morning dragged by with no word from him. Then I heard the news that there was a terrible fire at the Stoddard house the night before and for a brief moment I hoped it had consumed Kristen."
She scratched her cheek. "Strange how we can even think such things." She smoothed her skirt a few times from the middle over her legs and then tucked it under her.

"At around noon, Chief Williams showed up. He told me the whole family was dead. Then he told me the parents were found dead in their beds and the children were dead in their room, two of them just behind the door as though they were trying to escape the room but were unable to. The baby was just a lump of coal in its crib. At that point, they hadn't done any autopsies so they didn't know the mother and father had been shot, but they knew it was arson because the strength and quickness of the fire told them there was some kind of accelerant used.

Mrs. Covey stopped and took a breath.

"It didn't occur to me for a number of minutes that it was odd Chief Williams should be coming to my house to tell me about a fire at someone else's home. Probably I was so stunned by the recent events I was not processing much of what was happening to me. But, then he told me what he came to tell me. Kristen was not among the victims. She was seen around the time of the fire in the passenger seat of a dark green Falcon heading out of town, a black man behind the wheel."

A vision of the motel came back into my mind. The motel and the parking lot.

"Was that car," I asked slowly, "the car at the motel, was it a green Falcon?"

Mrs. Covey slowly clapped her hands, once, twice.

"Bravo!" She dropped her hands back into her lap. "Yeah, it was that very same car. Oh, and it gets worse. Chief Williams handed me a piece of paper." She got up abruptly and walked to a hutch across the room, opened the top drawer and pulled out a thin green, almost translucent paper.

"I can't believe I just left it there all this time. I should have burned it."

She made a little snort. "Here." She gave me the paper.

"I can't read," I told her, surprising myself that I admitted that so easily to her.

She didn't comment but took the paper and read the words out loud as she ran her finger just under the bottom of the letters.

"Sold. 1992 Falcon, two door, green. $500. Paid in full. Cash. To Rubin Covey."

She crossed back to the couch and seated herself.

She looked at me. "And then they were gone."

****

Mrs. Covey sent me back out to the Chief with sandwiches she made with white bread, cheese, and bologna. She was a nice lady. Much as she was mad with Chief Williams for hounding her about her husband's whereabouts and mad at me for taking up with Charlene, she didn't hold it against us that much.

"I believed in my husband's character for over thirty years," she told me, "so I guess I can't get all righteous with you for not figuring out Kristen's true nature in just three." She handed me the bag with the lunches. "But, now that you are hearing the truth about her from us who knew her, don't waste any more of your time on that girl. You're a nice man, I can see you mean well, and you got to realize you are the kind of guy that gets taken advantage of by people like her."

She gave me a little hug. She could see I wasn't totally convinced. "I'll be here if you need to come back."

I opened the door to the police cruiser and got in.

"Thanks, Mrs. Covey," I yelled out before I closed the car door.

She waved at me as we pulled away. I placed the sandwiches on the seat between me and the Chief. "Sandwiches," I told him.

He smiled over at me. "Nice lady."

I was puzzled.

"Then why do you keep bothering her?"

"It's my job, Hutchins. I can't let my liking of the woman keep me from getting to the bottom of this case. I got a fugitive out there, a dangerous one, and I have to keep on it until he is brought in."

He glanced over at me.

"So, you and Mrs. Covey have a nice talk?"

"Yes. She told me what happened."
"And?"
I knew what he wanted to hear.
"And I still don't know Rubin Covey."
We pulled into a space marked "Police Vehicles Only" in front of the station where we had gotten to know each other. I was suddenly felt very sleepy. Either being up all night had caught up with me or I didn't want to deal with any more of the Chief's interrogation.
"Come on, Hutchins." He grabbed up the sandwich bag and got out of the car. "I have a nice cell you can take a nap in."
I didn't know whether to thank him or start worrying, but I was too tired to care.

****

I must have slept all afternoon because when I woke up in the cell, I was starving and there was a plate with two of the sandwiches on it. I sat on my cot, ate my sandwiches, and wondered what to do next. I didn't see anyone around and wondered if the Chief was going to let me out when I asked him. And then what?
I got up and stood by the door and look through the bars. I wondered how Charlene could stand being locked up day after day. Strangely, she had never complained about being in jail. Maybe she knew she belonged there. Maybe, in spite of saying she dreamt about me and our home, she could take it or leave it. Maybe I cared more about us then she ever did.

****

The bars were cold in my hands. They sent a shiver down my spine. Something occurred to me that never had before. When the Sheriff took me off to jail, Charlene didn't say anything. She didn't tell him I hadn't killed the old man. She didn't say anything until the Sheriff came back with me and she knew he knew she did it.

I heard a door slam.
"Chief?" I called out. I tried to see down the hall but I couldn't see more than four feet down the gray cement wall.
"Chief?"
I heard another door slamming and then Chief Williams face appeared in front of me and he was putting a key in the cell door. I heard the tumblers click and the heavy door swung open.
"Come on," he motioned to me and I followed him down the hall.
"Freshen up," he said pointing to a bathroom at the end. "We're going to church."
"Church?"
"Yeah, wash up. You want answers? This is Kristen's church where her daddy was a deacon. It's a Saturday night service and there should be a good bunch of folks showing up that can tell you about Kristen and the family."
I stepped into the bathroom and turned the cold water on. I scrubbed my hands and washed my face. I hoped I didn't smell.
We walked down the street to the church that was God's home and everyone else's.
"What happens in the church?" I asked him.
"Happens? Just a normal service....one hour...short sermon, songs and prayer time."
"Am I supposed to do something?" I asked nervously.
Chief Williams stopped in the middle of the street we were crossing.
"Haven't you ever been to church before?"
"No." We had one in Whitfield Glen opposite the town office and I would see people dressed up on Sundays coming in or out and socializing in the small parking lot on the side of the building, but I never had the nerve to go in and nobody ever asked me.
The Chief whistled a low note.
"Well, that's a first. I never met a person who's never been to church before."

He started walking again and I lagged behind him by a step or two. "Never been to church," he repeated.

"Don't worry. You just sit. If you want to pray, you just put your hands together and close your eyes. After the service, you can talk to whoever is willing to conversate with you."

We arrived a couple of minutes later. Dropping my head and looking directly in front of me, I followed the Chief into the church. I was relieved to find folks weren't wearing fancy outfits, just regular day clothes, so I didn't stick out so badly.

It was pretty inside. It reminded me of Mrs. Covey's living room but it had long wooden benches with backs and golden cushions. The Chief and I sat in the third row, in the middle, with a family to either side of us, one with a boy and a girl in jeans and the other with twin girls dressed in matching black dresses with pink bows. I looked around the church and I saw mostly white faces, but there were some black faces, and a couple of families that looked like they came from one of those tropical places. The pastor stood up at a box in the front decorated with a sash with little yellow crosses hanging from it. There was a lady sitting at a small organ and seven ladies and two men standing in a group next to it.

Music started playing and the group began singing. All the people stood up with a book in their hands. The Chief motioned for me to stand, too, and he held his book in between us. I kept my mouth shut because I didn't know the words and the squiggles on the pages in front of me just looked like ants. But the song was surely pretty and it made me smile. Maybe this was the heaven people always talked about.

The hour went by too fast. I would have been happy to just sit there all evening listening to the music and the stories the pastor told about Jesus watching us and helping us and promising to give us what we wanted and needed. Then it got quiet and people bowed their heads and put their hands together. Some had their palms together and others wove their fingers together. I made a little round house with my hands and asked for Jesus to help me and Charlene. I made up my own little story when my eyes were shut and in it Charlene was the girl I remembered and not the one that showed up the day of the fire that got me locked up.

When I opened my eyes, I saw the Chief standing in the place where the pastor had been.

"Ladies and gentlemen," he said, "I am going to make a bit of a strange request of you today and I would like you to remember that you are Christians who are required by God to love one another, even those we don't quite understand." When he said "understand" he looked directly at me.

"We have a visitor today who has come here from Arkansas seeking some answers and some peace in his life. He has a good heart." Chief Williams paused and pointed me out and I wondered that he trusted me now because he was saying good things about me.

He continued. "This man lived a quiet life up in the mountains and one day a girl came to him, lost and destitute, and he gave her a home to stay in. He didn't ask her too many questions, just opened up his house and heart, giving her a safe place to settle. You may know that girl. Her name is Kristen Stoddard."

A collective gasp went up inside the church and all the heads turned to look at me. I dropped my head so I wouldn't have to see their faces. Chief Williams cleared his throat.

"Kristen Stoddard is in jail now in Mr. Hutchins' home town awaiting trial." I waited for him to say she had killed again but he didn't mention it.

"Mr. Hutchins just wants a few questions answered about Kristen. He came all the way here for your help. If you can spare a few moments of your time, I will be with Mr. Hutchins in the side sanctuary."

The church was dead silent.

"Thank you," he said and he stepped down from the podium and came to stand by the end of my row. The family next to me turned away and quickly filed out in front of me and headed for the church door. I stepped out into the aisle after them and Chief Williams took me by the arm and

led me to a little room with a small statue of Jesus on a cross and a circle of chairs. It was a pretty room that I would enjoy sitting in if just to stare at the pretty colorful windows with the hundreds of pieces of glass put together in a way that made pictures, but my heart was thumping and I wished I could just run out the door, out of the church, and have Mickey pick me up on the highway.

We sat down next to each other facing the open door to the big worship room and watched as the crowd got smaller and smaller. Finally, the pastor came in and five others came in after him. Two were white men, two were black men, and there was one white lady.

No one said anything for a minute. Then, one of the white men looked at me suspiciously and said, "So you were keeping Kristen with you, taking care of her, while her parents and babies lay in the cemetery.

I felt ashamed. The Chief spoke up. "He didn't know, Jim, he didn't know."

Jim didn't back down. He asked the question about Charlene being in jail in Whitfield Glen that the Chief didn't talk about.

"What did she do that got her arrested in Arkansas?"

The Chief spoke up for me again.

"Let's just say Kristen got in some trouble there."

Jim muttered, "I bet."

Thelady spoke up. She looked to be the age Charlene's parents would have been.

"What does Mr. Hutchins want to know?"

The moment had finally come and I wasn't sure now what it was I did want to know.

"I...I...," the words wouldn't come out of my mouth. "I...I......I just want to know...," and then I knew what I needed to know. "I just want to know if Char...Kristen...was always bad."

The pastor spoke first.

"I wouldn't say she was always bad, Mr. Hutchins. She was a lovely little girl if I remember correctly. She used to like to help put flowers in the

church and when she got to be about eleven or twelve, she would run errands for some of our elderly parishioners."

"And she did babysit my kids when she turned twelve," the lady broke in. I notice she flinched a little but then she said, "My children always liked her and she treated the kids well."

Jim grunted. "Yeah, and then she got pregnant. She was all of thirteen. She was hell after that on her family. I remember her daddy telling me she would sneak out and lie and wouldn't even tell him which boys she was running with."

The other white man spoke up. "That's when the Stoddards started homeschooling. They were too embarrassed to have their daughter showing up with her big belly in school."

The pastor sighed. "Yes, it was a very difficult time for Thomas and Mary. Why Mary stopped coming to church even though most folks tried to be kindly toward her. She hardly left the house except to go to her sister's for weekends over in New Freedom. I guess that's how she escaped the problems she was having with Kristen."

The lady said, "Yes, she left Thomas to handle Kristen and keep her in line, keep her from going out and getting pregnant again."

"Yeah, he didn't have much luck with that," the other white man said. "For all his locking the house down, she still found a way to get around him."

I had one more question. My voice shook. "So why did she do what she did?"

The pastor clasped his hands together and pressed them against his mouth.

"We can't know just why, Mr. Hutchins. Sometimes when people start going down a path of deceit and ruin, they take everyone with them. All we have ever been able to gather was that Kristen wanted what she wanted and when she decided to run away with Rubin Covey, she eliminated everything that stood in her way. She must have lost whatever flame of compassion she had when she was younger. Her parents and her

children, they must just have become a problem for her and she found a way to solve her problem by erasing them from her world."

Jim blurted out, "Psycho. That's what she is."

I didn't have anything more to ask. All I knew was Charlene was once nice and then she was not. I thought it would make me feel better to know she had been good sometime earlier in her life, but now it just made me feel sadder. I wished I could have been in Jenkins when she was thirteen. Maybe I could have been enough to her then to keep her from going bad.

Chief Williams stood up. "Thanks. All of you. I am sure Mr. Hutchins appreciated your willingness to come forward and speak with him."

I nodded. "Thanks." It came out more like a whisper.

As we all stood up, the pastor came over and put his hands on my shoulders.

"Son," he said in his deep voice, "Remember God works in mysterious ways. I don't know why Kristen came into your life, but maybe there was something you learned from your experience with her."

I thought about the two nice years I had with Charlene and wondered how it helped that God gave me a nice present and then took it away from me.

"And something brought you here to us, Mr. Hutchins. Maybe there is something in that."

He smiled at me and took his hands from my shoulders.

I looked past him into the pretty church. It was true I never had been away from home and I had met some nice people here and I liked coming to the church service.

We started to leave the room when one of the black men finally spoke.

He was baldheaded, about seventy. He peered into my face curiously.

He spoke to the other black man.

"Ain't he the spitting image of Cesford Covey? Rubin Covey's great uncle?"

The air suddenly sucked out of the room.

Chief Williams spun around.

"What did you say, Albert?"

Albert straightened up and wagged his arthritic finger at me.
"He looks just like Cesford Covey, I swear. Wasn't he from Arkansas,
Willie?" he asked glancing over his shoulder at his friend.
The look the Chief gave me could have chilled a bowl of chicken soup in
August.
He turned and strode out of the church without another word to me.
I slowly walked stiff-legged down the aisle to the door and out alone onto
the street. My head felt empty. I looked up at the night sky and the stars
were hidden behind the clouds. I knew they were there, but like the truth,
there didn't seem to be any way to find them, make them show their faces.
I felt a tug at my jacket sleeve.
"Mr. Hutchins?" The girl belonging to the hand pulling at my elbow spoke
in a tiny voice which matched her small frame and the wisps of brown
hair that curved around her head like a Christmas wreath.
"I was Kristen's friend."
I started to turn away. I didn't really want to hear any more. There was
no point.
"Please," she insisted and when I turned back, she smiled a little.
"I just want to tell you that Kristen didn't go crazy until her father started
locking her up. They way the others tell it, she was causing problems that
made Mr. Stoddard have to be real strict with her. But, I don't remember
it that way. Kristen sort of disappeared one day, stopped hanging out with
me, and then next I saw her she was pregnant. I tried to talk to her but
she told me to go away and leave her alone."
The girl looked paler than she had when I first saw her.
"I was a stupid teenager and I was mad at her for giving me the cold
shoulder and I never bothered with her again."
She opened her purse and took out a tiny rectangle.
"I kept this all these years in my wallet." She handed it to me. "Here. You
take it."
She snapped her purse shut. "Maybe I could have been a better friend," she
said. Then she turned away from me and walked off.

I started walking toward the police department building, looking at the little picture of Charlene. She must have been maybe twelve or thirteen in it. Her eyes were bright, her hair shiny and falling in big waves over her shoulders. She was smiling like she was really happy. I wondered what happened to that Charlene. I got to the building and I slid the picture into my pocket.

I pushed open the door and walked straight to the police chief's office. He was sitting in his chair waiting for me like a hungry lion. He immediately rose to his feet.

"You, Mr. Hutchins who-never-knew-Rubin Covey...," he said with a good deal of sarcasm, "You will be gracing my jail for another night." He shoved me down the hall, opened the lock noisily, and put me inside the cell. He looked at me and shook his head.

"I don't know what game you are playing but you almost had me, Mr. Hutchins."

He slammed the door, stomped down the corridor and hit the light switch. Except for a tiny light by the commode in the corner of the cell, I was in the dark. I curled into a ball on the cot and hoped I could just stay that way forever.

****

I only had a few minutes of peace. My mind started whirring, thoughts jumping all around, scenes of Charlene and me back at the house, Charlene with her fake mother, Charlene as the pretty little girl in the photo, Charlene giving a blow job to the jailer.

Then I saw the pretty church and Mrs. Covey's house. I wished I could spend more time in her home, watching her cook in the kitchen, sitting in her "parlour" being given tea. I imagined how it might be if Chief Williams wasn't mad at me and we could sit and talk some more about anything that didn't have to do with Charlene and her lover, Rubin Covey.

Rubin Covey, Cesford Covey, I didn't know them. But, then I never knew anyone. I just knew my mother was Bess Hutchins and my daddy was Clifford Hutchins and my aunt and uncle, they were Hutchins, too. I never heard any other names but Hutchins.

I don't know when I finally fell asleep but I was glad I did. Chief Williams came to my cell right at 8:00 am. He didn't say good morning.

I got up from my cot and looked him right in his face.

"I want to go see Mrs. Covey," I said, my voice steady and sure.

He nodded, just barely, and we walked in silence out of the building. We rode over to her house without saying a word.

When I opened the door to get out, he said, "When you're finished here, you walk back to the station." He looked at me with his dark eyes, unblinking. "If you skip town before I tell you I'm finished with you, I'll put a warrant out for your arrest. Do you understand?"

I didn't have to answer. I closed the car door and walked up the steps to Mrs. Covey's front door. I knocked lightly, and then harder, until she came half-asleep to the door.

Her hair was in a pink hair net and she had a thick robe tied around her pajamas. Her feet were bare and I noticed her toes were crooked. Her face pulled together like a crumpled napkin and she said, "What the hell are you doing here at this hour? Mercy," she huffed but she took one look at my crusty face and let me in.

"What's ailing you?" she asked. "And why did the Chief dump you at my door and speed off like that?"

I told her what happened at the church and that someone said I was a Covey or looked like a Covey.

"Let me get dressed," she said, and when she came back, she made us some coffee and gave me a piece of apple Danish warmed up.

She took charge. "Okay. Let's get to the bottom of this. Come on into the basement room and we'll start looking through the boxes I haven't been into for years. They got all kinds of family stuff, photos, birth certificates.

Maybe we will find that missing link between you and Rubin before the Chief comes back and charges you with obstruction of justice and arrests you for aiding and abetting a wanted man." She harrumphed which I didn't quite get the meaning of any more than I understood all that law language that probably just meant jail for me.

Mrs. Covey opened up a big storage closet and told me to start hauling boxes out. We pulled apart the tucked in cardboard on the top of the boxes and started going through the Covey history.

"This is my grandmother, Beatrice," she said. "Her last name was Thompson." She raised her eyebrows at me. I shook my head. "Well, probably we can skip my side of the family. You are supposed to be related to Rubin." The sound of his name made me uncomfortable, but, I was going to hear it over and over again throughout the morning.

"Rubin's aunt, Geraldine Crooks."

"Rubin's uncle, Carroll. He lived out in Georgia."

"Oh, here, is something interesting. It's a letter from Bridgeport, Arkansas." Mrs. Covey opened it and pulled out a sheet of paper. "Oh, never mind. This was from my sister when she went there for a teaching job for three months."

"Rubin's.....now, I don't know who this is." She handed me a picture of some man with bushy hair. He didn't look like anyone I had ever known. We went through eight boxes by 11 am. All the Covey's were starting to look the same to me. So far none of them had my face. We found no birth certificates or marriage certificates or wills from Whitfield Glen or any other place in Arkansas. We didn't find any stuff about this great-uncle of Rubin, this Cesford Covey. By the time we were on the ninth box, I felt like I knew the Coveys real well.

Mrs. Covey hesitated before she opened the last box. She placed her hands on top of it like she was either giving it a blessing or she was not going to let out whatever was inside. There were some words written on the outside in black magic marker and a red heart with an arrow through it.

"What is it?" I asked.

Mrs. Covey took her hands away from the box top and turned the box to the side with the heart and writing.

"It says Rubin and Alma. That's me," she pointed at herself. "Alma."

She pulled open the top.

"Thirty years," she said under her breath. "And it all comes down to this."

And she looked at me as though I was the one carrying the plague, the Kristen plague.

She handed me a black-and-white photo.

"That's us on our first date."

Mrs. Covey and Rubin stood side by side in clothes that would have made me laugh under some other circumstance. They looked nice together. They were smiling and gazing at each other. You could tell they were in love. She handed me another one.

She didn't need to explain. She was wearing a white wedding dress in it. Rubin seemed happy to be marrying her. He had a big grin on his face, white teeth gleaming into the camera.

She handed me one picture after the other, glancing at it and then letting me take a look. We made a stack of them on the floor. I didn't see any pictures of children.

"I couldn't have any," she said and I didn't ask anything more about that. The Covey's faces grew older in the pictures as we worked our way toward the bottom of the box.

"I was in a mood one day," she told me, "and I realized that our story started at the end if the newest pictures were on the top. So I took them all out and put the recent ones at the bottom." She sighed. "Funny, I did that just before the fire, like I knew there wasn't going to be any reason to add any more pictures anyhow."

We became quieter as we got into their last year together. Rubin was still smiling, though, in every picture, like he didn't have a care in the world and there was nothing going on that would ruin everyone's life.

There were just a few photos left scattered on the cardboard bottom.

Mrs. Covey pulled out the largest one and handed it to me.

"Our last summer together," she said bitterly. "We took a picnic to the river. Rubin acted like he was twenty years old again, singing to me, and chasing me in and out of the trees, well, as fast as we could run at our age."

Her voice softened and she stared off toward the ceiling, lost in the memory of Rubin when he wasn't the creep he had become.

I looked down at the photo. They were all smiles as usual. Rubin didn't have much hair left and Mrs. Covey's black hair had a good amount of gray in it. The sun glinted off their faces....must have been after they had their romping about.

"Billy Ray?"

I felt like I was stuck in a place where there was no time.

I felt giddy.

"Billy Ray?" Mrs. Covey was shaking me. I wondered if she would slap me on the side of the head like she had done at our first meeting.

"Billy Ray? What is it?"

I blinked and stared at the photo again.

"Do you recognize Rubin, Billy Ray?"

I shook my head no.

I pointed to his teeth.

"Mrs. Covey? Are they real?"

"What?" She started laughing. "His teeth? Goodness, I thought you had seen a ghost, Billy Ray!"

"Are the real?" I asked her again.

"Hell, no! Who around here has their real teeth past the age of fifty?"

"Did Mr. Stoddard have false teeth too?" I found myself staring at Mrs. Covey's teeth.

"Well, heck, I don't know," she said. "Probably. Maybe. What's gotten into you?"

I breathed in once, twice. I pointed to Rubin Covey's mouth.

"He's got a chip in his tooth under his right cheek."

Mrs. Covey shrugged. "Yeah, he chipped one of his denture teeth on a bottle cap he was twisting off in his mouth. He didn't want to pay to have it fixed."

"You know that man Char...Kristen...killed in Arkansas?"

Mrs. Covey nodded and waited.

"He had false teeth just like this. He had a chip right there, too," and I pointed to the spot again.

Mrs. Covey looked confused.

"Are you saying that man was Rubin?" She squinched up her nose and she fought to remember the details. "Didn't you say it was some old white man Kristen had a run in with just before she met you?"

I nodded. "Yeah, he was white."

Mrs. Covey wasn't understanding what I was trying to get at. I wasn't too sure myself; it was still stuck in the back of my mind, like those stars hiding behind the clouds.

I looked at Rubin's teeth in the photo and I could see those teeth in that skeleton in the photo Mr. Stanley had forced me to look at. They were the same teeth. I knew they were.

I got to my knees and then stood up, holding the picture in my hand.

"We gotta go see Chief Williams."

Mrs. Covey looked at me strangely, but went and got her coat, purse, and keys.

She didn't stick to the speed limit.

****

Chief Williams was talking to one of his men just inside the lobby of the building. He stopped abruptly when he saw the two of us come in and pushed the officer away.

He put his hands on his hips.

"Did you find your lost relative, Hutchins?"

I walked right up to him.

"I need you to call Sheriff Hathaway in Whitfield Glen."

He got a puzzled look and seemed like he was about to cuss me out, but then he changed his mind.

I must have looked real serious.

"Let's go to my office." The Chief led us back through the door with the silver rectangle on it and seated us in the two chairs opposite his desk.

I sat there with the picture clutched between my hands. He reached over for it and pulled it out of my grip.

He didn't look impressed.

"It's Rubin and Alma."

"Please, call the Sheriff."

He picked up the phone, talked to information, and told them to put him through to the Sheriff's Department in Whitfield Glen.

I looked over at Mrs. Covey. She was sitting like a statue or someone who had accidentally gotten on a bus, didn't know where it was going, and couldn't get off.

The Chief had gotten through.

"This is Police Chief Williams over in Jenkins, Tennessee. I need to speak to the Sheriff." There was about a minute of silence.

"Sheriff? This is Police Chief Williams calling you from Jenkins, Tennessee. I am with one Billy Ray Hutchins...yeah, I said Billy Ray Hutchins...well, yes, he came in yesterday, no, the day before yesterday, asking a whole bunch of questions about Kristen Stoddard."

I reached across the table and waved my hand under the Chief's face.

"What?" he barked at me. "Wait one minute, Sheriff, Billy Ray is...what is it, Billy Ray?"

"Can you send him the picture?" I asked.

The Chief threw up his hands. "Is there a purpose in this, Hutchins? Apparently, you're not going to tell me." He pushed the mouthpiece back under his chin. "Sheriff? You got a fax number? Uh...huh...okay...," he scribbled on a notepad. "Could you hold on for that, Sheriff?" He put the phone down on the desk, got up and opened the door.

"Ramirez? Rameeeerez!"

An officer probably named Ramirez appeared and the Chief handed him the photo and the number he had scribbled down and told the officer to fax it right away.

He sat back down and picked up the phone.

"Okay, Sheriff, it's coming to you now."

We waited a few minutes.

"You got it? Yeah, it's a photo of the guy in the newspaper who Kristin ran off with...ah, yeah, that's his wife."

He glanced up momentarily at Mrs. Covey but she didn't move a muscle.

He looked over at me.

"And?"

"Tell the Sheriff to go find the picture of that burned up skull of the old man that Charlene...Kristen...killed."

The Chief shook his head at me but repeated what I said to the Sheriff.

We sat in silence, the Chief leaning on his left elbow, holding the phone up to his ear. He gazed over my head at the wall behind me.

I saw him sit up a little and his eyes widened a bit.

"Holy Shit! You gotta be kidding me! What the hell?"

He shook his head violently. His voice got loud.

"What friggin' DNA tests on the corpses? You think we have money for that here in Jenkins? Hell, did you do DNA tests on your corpse? I didn't damn well think so. Besides, we had no question. They were husband and wife, together in their bed. Covey was seen in the car with Kristen. It was Kristen and a black man. No, it was two people who testified to that. No, they didn't see the black man. It was night. They saw a man that was dark enough not to look white."

He was standing up now, pacing back and forth in the space between the desk and his chair.

Chief Williams rubbed his free hand from his hairline down over his chin. He couldn't stop shaking his head.

"Goddamn it to hell! No wonder we couldn't find Covey and Kristen. There was no Covey and Kristen. No black guy, white girl. Shit! Goddamn it! Shit!"

He finally stopped swearing and dropped back down into his chair. "Yeah, yeah, we're on our way, Sheriff. It will be worth the trip." He hung up the phone.

He cocked his head and looked at me. "You figured this out? You?" I didn't say anything and suddenly the Chief became aware of Mrs. Covey again, sitting stone still in front of him.

He bit his lip.

"Mrs. Covey," he said softly. "Your husband...Rubin...he didn't run away with Kristen."

Mrs. Covey gave him a blank stare.

The Chief started over.

"Mrs. Covey, your husband hasn't been on the run for the last four years. He died that night in the fire at the Stoddard's. I don't know why he was there but he was the man who was killed, not Kristen's father. Her father was the one that drove off with her.

Mrs. Covey found her voice just a little bit. "But, there was a black man in the car with Kristen, wasn't that what people said?"

Chief Williams nodded.

"Yes and no. The witnesses saw Kristen and they knew it was her. But the man just appeared not to be white to them. All I can figure at this point is that Mr. Stoddard wiped soot on his face to disguise himself, to make people think he was the one killed in the fire and Rubin was the one taking off with Kristen."

Mrs. Covey whispered softly, "Then my Rubin is dead?" "Yes, Mrs. Covey."

"Dead." You could tell she was having trouble fixing that idea in her head. "He was dead all along. And all these years I've been mad at him for killing those kids and running away. And he didn't do it." Her voice started breaking. "Maybe he was still a sinner for messing with that young

girl but at least he wasn't no baby killer." The tears were spilling down her cheeks now and as she sat there and sobbed and muttered her husband's name over and over, the Chief and I got lost in our own thoughts.

****

I never knew a woman could cry for so long but Mrs. Covey had a whole lot to cry about so she didn't stop for the better part of an hour. Finally, she ran out of energy and tears, and the Chief got up and helped her from her chair.

Before we left the office, Chief Williams told us he was heading to Arkansas to talk with the Sheriff and compare notes. He wanted to talk to Charlene too.

He looked at me.

"I assume you want a ride back, Hutchins?" He wasn't actually asking me a question, just stating a fact.

"Mrs. Covey?" He took one of her hands. "Normally, I wouldn't do this, but I feel I owe you a bit of an apology for dogging you these last years over where Rubin was. So, if you would like to go along for the ride to Arkansas, you are welcome to come. The department will cover the hotel bill when we get to Whitfeld Glen."

She nodded immediately.

"I want to go. Now I am like Billy Ray here. I need answers and maybe I will find them in Arkansas."

Chief Williams laughed, not at Mrs. Covey, but just because he couldn't believe what was happening.

"Strangest damn case I've ever seen," he said later that afternoon as we piled into the police cruiser. Mrs. Covey sat up front and I sat behind her. I was lucky it was the Chief's car and was one of those fancy unmarked ones or I would have been riding in the cage.

"Let's go," he said, and we headed west on Route 40 and in three or four hours I would be home. As we started, I wasn't really sure I wanted to get there considering I didn't know what had changed for the better.

Charlene was still a killer and everyone around her was still dead. Maybe when I meet Charlene this time, I will see her for what she is, the twenty-one-year-old bad Charlene - I think that is her age now - and I will just come back to Jenkins and forget she ever existed.

****

VI

"I don't understand something!" Mrs. Covey blurted out an hour into the trip.
"What was Stoddard doing with my husband's false teeth?"
Chief Williams chuckled.
"I would guess he took them out of Rubin's mouth because he didn't want to leave anything that would be easily recognized or traced. But why he decided to use them himself, your guess is as good as mine. Dentures are fitted to a person's mouth so wearing somebody else's usually doesn't work out too well. Maybe Stoddard just got lucky and they fit good. Must have lost his own somewhere along the way."
"By the way," the Chief looked over his right shoulder at me. "What's up with your Rubin connection?"
"We didn't find a thing," I told him.
"I can vouch for that," said Mrs. Covey. "We spent the whole morning going through Rubin's family tree and nothing fell out and landed on Billy Ray."
"Huh."
Chief Williams dropped the subject which surprised me.
We passed over the Mississippi River from Tennessee to Arkansas about six o'clock. We stopped for a little dinner and after getting our stomachs a bit full, Mrs. Covey fell asleep. We could hear her snoring just a little bit every minute or so.
"Billy Ray."
I lifted my head up from where it had settled on the window.
"Yeah, Chief?"
This time Chief Williams didn't look over at me but looked straight ahead at the road.
"I'm going to be straight with you. I still have a murder investigation that's my responsibility. Don't get the impression that just because I can be

friendly toward you that I am not paying attention to what you do." He glanced in the rear view mirror and his eyes met mine for a moment. "Right now, the only suspect in the Stoddard family murders and the murder of Rubin Covey is Kristen. She is also the only suspect in the murder of Mr. Stoddard. The guy that we thought was Kristen partner's in crime is dead. The guy that was Kristin's actual partner, her father, is also dead because she made sure of that."

I was trying to follow what he was saying but I was losing where he was at.

He glanced at me again. "Do you know what that means, Hutchins?"

I figured he was going to tell me.

"You, Billy Ray, are the only one outside Kristen with a connection to the murders in both Jenkins and Whitfeld Glen. And that picture of Rubin Covey with your names on it connects you to both crimes and Covey and Kristen."

"So, how is it," he asked me, "that you expect me to believe you just innocently got stuck in the middle?"

I shrugged my shoulders and stared out the window.

"I tell you what I think. I think, Billy Ray, you are about the most honest man I have ever met." He grinned at me in the mirror.

"I've been going over this ever since we left Jenkins and all I can come up with is that you really had no idea what was heading your way when Kristen showed up. I am on your side now, Billy Ray, which is why I am going to give you a little advice."

Chief Williams turned off the highway into the service area and pulled into a parking space next to some picnic tables.

"Come out and sit with me for a minute, Billy Ray."

I was worried that we shouldn't leave Mrs. Covey sleeping in the car.

"She'll be fine. We'll just sit here at the picnic table. Let her get some more rest."

We sat down on opposite sides on the pine benches. Chief Williams looked real serious. I didn't think I liked where this conversation was going to go.

Each mile nearer we got to Whitfeld Glen, the more my feelings for Charlene came back. I was starting to feel guilty that I ever thought of just staying in Jenkins, leaving her all alone with no one to look in on her. Once I believed in Charlene and our love and I thought that there must be something in her that made me not give up on her.

Of course, when I was in Jenkins, the people I met made me see that the Charlene I loved stopped existing at thirteen-years-old. She became selfish and cruel and violent and a coldblooded killer.

But, now that I was half way home, I was half way in between loving Charlene and hating her.

"Billy Ray," began Chief Williams, "I don't know how you are feeling about Kristen now. I think you are probably confused about her. You have heard the bad things, and some good things...well, mostly bad things, but you are probably remembering your good times with her."

He must have been reading my mind.

"Now when you walk back into that jail in Whitfeld Glen, you are likely going to forget everything you heard in Jenkins because you will just see Kristen, the only girl you have ever loved."

I studied a knot in the pine table and started tracing it with my thumb.

"Billy Ray, look at me."

I made myself look up.

"Billy Ray, Kristen has committed crimes in two death penalty states. If one state doesn't kill her, the other will. Murdering three little children, her mother, Rubin Covey, and her father in such a horrible ways won't exactly inspire juries to go easy on her. One of the things the Sheriff and I are going to be discussing is where she should be tried first and in which state she should be imprisoned. Either way it ends up, Kristen is going to be on death row and, one day, the state will do what is required and Kristen will be executed."

I flinched. I never really thought of Charlene as not coming home, even when I was in the middle of being angry with her and not trusting her.

Now Chief Williams was telling me it didn't matter if I loved her or not. She was going to be taken away from me.

"Guard your heart, Billy Ray. Walk away now. Go to your home when we get to town. Don't come to the jail. Then, when we're finished, let us come and get you and bring you back to Jenkins. When Kristen has the baby, I will work with the courts to see that the baby is brought to you and we will find some way, and someone, to help you raise it."

"Why can't I stay with Charlene until the baby comes?"

The Chief spoke very clearly and slowly, like he thought I wasn't going to understand.

"If you stay with her, Billy Ray, when the baby comes, the courts are going to deem that you are not fit to be a father, even with help, because you chose to support a woman who murdered her last three children. You can have your "Charlene" or you can have your baby, but you can't have both."

He reached out and grabbed my arm.

"Once she's convicted, there is not a thing you can do for her. You will essentially be on death row with her. But, your baby, you can give a life to, Billy Ray, a life. Don't make a mistake with this."

I knew he was right, but I didn't know if I would have the strength to turn away from her.

****

Mrs. Covey was still asleep when we got back in the car and she stayed that way all the way to Whitfeld Glen. The sun was just setting as we arrived and the town already looked like it was ready to get into bed. We were parked across from the jail and I could see the Sheriff was waiting for us, his cruiser parked directly in front of the building. I noticed for the first time how small and dull Main Street looked when I compared it to Jenkins. It seemed almost like some old shoes that you didn't realize was so tore up until someone gave you a new pair.

"We here?" asked Mrs. Covey picking her head up from her chest.

"Yes, Ma'am, we are," said Chief Williams, "but, before we go in to meet with the Sheriff, I want to know if you would like a ride up to your house, Billy Ray." He nodded yes to me and waited for me to accept his offer. I started to say something, but instead I reached for the door handle and jumped out of the car.

"Shit!" I heard from the window as I ran across the street and into the jail before the Chief could stop me.

"Go on into my office, Billy Ray," Sheriff Hathaway told me and he ordered his deputy to take me there. I had been there the time I got arrested for killing the old man. A few minutes later, the Chief and Mrs. Covey came in and the Sheriff pulled a third chair in from the room next door. He closed the door behind him.

"Well, Billy Ray," he said, "you have become quite the traveling man, a knight in shining armor fighting dragons for his lady."

I knew he was making fun of me.

Then, Chief Williams spoke up.

"Can I see that skull picture you have from the crime scene?" he asked the Sheriff.

"Sure." Sheriff Hathaway passed over the photo. The Chief compared the two pictures, the one from the crime and the one with the picture of Rubin.

"I wanted to see this for myself, Sheriff. It's a definite match."

Mrs. Covey learned over and looked at the pictures herself. She took in a sharp breath when her eyes shifted over to the picture of the burned up skull with her husband's dentures in it.

Chief Williams looked over at Sheriff Hathaway.

"You know, the change of victim here rather throws a wrench into the motives we assigned up until now. We always thought, back in Jenkins, that Rubin Covey got caught up with a promiscuous girl who was tired of her parents' attempts to control her and sick of being forced to take care of her children day in and day out. We theorized that Rubin and Kristen planned to run away together. He had bought a car just a few days prior

and he drove over to the property that night. We thought he was trying to sneak out with her, leaving the children to be cared for by their grandparents, and taking off for parts unknown.

The Sheriff asked, "Did you figure it was more Rubin or more Kristen who hatched this escape plan?"

Mrs. Covey spoke up. "I always thought Kristen had to have been pulling the strings. I never could have children and Rubin always wanted some. I guarantee if the girl came with kids, he would have been fine with it."

"I tend to agree with Mrs. Covey," said the Chief. "It was often said by the Stoddard neighbors that Kristen didn't talk positively about her pregnancies or show off the children as most mothers would."

"Billy Ray?"

"Yeah?"

"Did Kristen ever talk to you about having children during the time you were together?"

I had to think about it for a minute but I don't remember her ever bringing up the subject.

"No. Never." I felt like a traitor to Charlene, telling them this.

The Chief went on. "So, we figured Rubin met with Kristen, drove her back over to her house and he thought Kristen would just run in the house, grab her stuff, and bolt out the door, but then her parents tried to stop her. The Stoddard's were the type to keep a loaded shotgun in the closet and Kristen knew that. We were able to get a couple prints off the shotgun that luckily had been tossed onto the lawn and they were both Kristen's."

I felt my chest tighten. I hadn't known that. I always figured Rubin killed them because he was the bad guy, well, except he wasn't quite so bad any more.

"Then," said the Chief, "in a panic, they looked for a way to cover up the crime. They grabbed a can of gasoline and started throwing gas over the bodies of the adults and all over the furniture."

"Why would they have killed the kids?" asked Sheriff Hathaway

"Hell if I know. I don't know how anyone can kill children. First we thought the fire just got out of control and the children got trapped in the room where they stayed with Kristen, all three of them in there together. But then our fire expert said that the gasoline was poured on the beds and the crib and splashed on the walls and that the door was bolted shut from the outside."

"Bolted shut?" Mrs. Covey cried out. "Oh, no, there is no way Rubin could ever have done such a thing!"

There was a silence in the room.

"No, you are right," said the Chief slowly. "We know now that Rubin wasn't involved in the crime and, if he were running off with Kristen, it doesn't make sense she would shoot him unless it was an accident."

"The bolts on the doors," the Sheriff repeated. "Who puts bolts on the outside of a door in the first place?"

I looked over at the Chief and he had a strange expression on his face. "I heard a rumor once that Mr. Stoddard put a bolt on Kristen's door to keep her from sneaking out of the house and getting herself knocked up. They have real high doors in the house with flat woodwork and the bolt we found," he stopped and thought, "was put on the top of the door, not the side, and it bolted down so you had to be pretty tall to pull the bolt into place. I always thought it was a pretty dangerous idea, locking someone in the room. How would you get out in case of fire?"

Someone knocked on the office door.

"Yeah, what is it?" yelled the Sheriff.

"There is a phone call for you on Line 2," the deputy said through the door.

"Tell them to call back."

"I think you may want to take this one, Sheriff. Some guy named Devon Covey says he has something to tell you about Rubin."

My mouth dropped open. Another Covey? Mrs. Covey waved her hand at the Sheriff. "Take the damn call!"

"Got it," he yelled back through the door. He looked at all of us. "I am going to put this on speaker phone."

He took the phone receiver off the hook, pressed the second button and an orange one to the right.

"Mr. Covey? This is Sheriff Hathaway. You wanted to tell me something?"

We heard a lot of static and then this Devon Covey's voice came out of the speaker.

"Yeah, well, I heard through a cousin of mine who heard from a friend of his about some crime Rubin was supposed to be involved in. I heard he was said to be catting around with some young girl and got himself into a jam and then nobody heard from him again. I was told you were having some meeting to discuss what he did and I just wanted to tell you what I heard, because what I heard was a different story."

"Go ahead," said the Sheriff.

"Well," the voice said, "What I heard was from my friend's friend - his name was Rodney - who worked with Rubin at the hospital. He said he warned Rubin not to get involved in other people's business but Rubin didn't listen to him and tried to help some girl out. Rodney said Rubin even went so far as to get the girl a car so she could take her children and skip town. One night he got in trouble with the boss because he left the hospital in the middle of the shift to meet the girl. Rodney thought he was just going out to get something on the side, but when Rubin came back he was freaked out. He was ranting and raving about how sick people were, how could they do things like that to a girl, and then he took a bunch of supplies - bandages and ointments and stuff - and left the hospital again. He got wrote up for stealing by the floor manager, but he never got in trouble for it because he never came back to the hospital again. Rodney didn't tell me all the rest of what happened, but I guess that's when Rubin disappeared. Rodney said he didn't even know for years because he had his own problems and he had gotten fired himself the next day and caught a bus to California where he was from."

I could hear Mrs. Covey sniffling besides me and wiping her eyes with both hands.

"Anything else, Mr. Covey?" asked the Sheriff.

"No, that's all I know."

"We thank you for making the call, Mr. Covey." The Sheriff looked over at Chief Williams.

"Oh, yeah, uh, Mr. Covey," said the Chief leaning toward the speaker. "I just have one question for you. Have you ever heard of a man by the name of Billy Ray Hutchins?"

"No."

"Okay, thank you, Mr. Covey."

The Sheriff hung up the phone.

The Chief looked over at me and grinned. "I had to ask. It's driving me nuts."

Then he smiled at Mrs. Covey, "Well, now you know your man always loved you. He was as good a man as you thought."

Mrs. Covey smiled through her tears, nodding her head.

My brain felt like it was melting. The whole picture of that horrible night kept changing and changing.

"Okay," said the Sheriff. "Let's see what we've got here."

"We've got Rubin Covey," said the Chief, "A rescuer, not a lover."

The Sheriff added to the story.

"And we've got a girl who seemingly planned to take her children with her when she left town."

"And we got something awful enough happening to that girl that she needed some form of medical attention...wait!" The Chief turned toward Mrs. Covey again. "The day you saw Rubin at the motel with Kristin...wasn't that exactly one day before the fire? Wasn't that on a Sunday?"

"Yeah, it was Sunday night."

"And Mrs. Stoddard would leave on the weekends to stay with her sister." The Sheriff stood up behind his desk and leaned on his chair.

"Jesus Christ! I wonder what went on in that locked room. It makes my stomach turn."

I finally spoke up.

"I was told no one really knew what boys...uh, Kristen...was going out to see or who she had those babies by."

Chief Williams was shaking his head.

"Gotta wonder if those were Mr. Stoddard's babies or if Kristen got pregnant by somebody he was putting in the room with her. Sick bastard."

"So," the Sheriff went back to that night, "You got Rubin trying to get Kristen out of there when he gets himself shot. She wouldn't shoot him if he was helping her. So why are Kristen's fingerprints on the shotgun?"

"Probably she was trying to get the gun away from her father."

The Chief agreed. "Makes sense."

"And once the one murder is committed, Stoddard can't leave witnesses, so he shoots his wife."

"Then," chimes in Chief Williams, "Stoddard decides to get rid of the kids because they are only a liability, so he goes into Kristen's bedroom where the children were asleep and he starts tossing gas over all over the place, lights a match...and the place goes up like a torch, fire rolling across the ceiling, everything becoming like a burning iron."

"And then closes the door and bolts it shut," said the Sheriff.

The room swum a bit before my eyes.

Sheriff Williams said, "The two older kids tried to get out because we found them just on the other side of the door."

"So, she didn't kill her kids?" asked Mrs. Covey.

Chief Williams looked like he had been hit with a brick. He kept blinking his eyes and you could see he was searching for just the right answer.

"Well, it's just a scenario, Mrs. Covey," said the Chief. "Kristen's fingerprints were on the shotgun, she ran town, and she killed a man in just the same way. If we had some evidence to back the theory, it would be another story."

*I felt my eyes fill up and then tears came down both my cheeks. I started
doing that thing where you breathe too fast and I began shaking
uncontrollably.*

"Billy Ray!"

*The Sheriff opened the door and yelled out to the officer on duty to bring a
paper bag pronto.*

*Mrs. Covey started rubbing my shoulders and then someone handed me
the paper bag and told me to put it around my mouth and breathe slowly.
I tried, gulping, and gulping, and the bag was getting wet, but, finally, I
stopped shaking and could breathe normally again.*

*"What the hell is it, Billy Ray? What's going on?" The Sheriff was leaning
down over me.*

"Go look at Charlene's fingers." I didn't get the last word out all the way.

"Her what?"

"Her fingers, her fingers."

*The Chief looked at the Sheriff and made a 'whatever' face and they went
out of the room together and down the hall.*

I sat there and tried not to hold my breath, trying to breathe normal.

We waited about ten minutes and then they came in back in the room.

Mrs. Covey looked at them, eager for an explanation.

The Chief looked at me and then her.

*"Every one of her fingertips is scarred. Not real noticeable, but, if you look
close, every one of them."*

*"We should have noticed that when she was fingerprinted," said the
Sheriff. "Maybe we did but it didn't ring any bells at the time."*

The Chief pulled a chair over next to me and sat down.

*"She must have tried like hell to save those children, to get that red-hot
bolt pulled back."*

*"My Charlene didn't do it, she didn't do it." I said over and over. It was
the only thing that really mattered.*

The Sheriff picked up the phone and dialed.

"Sorry to bother you, Mr. Dawson, at your dinner hour. I just want to tell you we are dropping the charges against Kristen Stoddard."
I felt something like an actually happy feeling coming up in me.
"Long story. I will explain it to you tomorrow."
He hung up the phone.
He looked over at me with a bit of a smirk.
"What jury is going to convict Kristen for giving Stoddard a dose of his own medicine? How would they know that she wasn't in fear of her life? That she didn't go temporarily insane when the murderer of her children showed up? That she wasn't trying to save your life, Billy Ray?" For the first time, the Sheriff actually smiled at me in a kind way.
I twisted around and looked at Chief Williams.
He was collecting his papers in a file folder.
"I can't see that there's any case in Tennessee that has anything to do with anyone here in Whitfeld Glen," he commented quietly.
The Sheriff opened the door and herded us out into the waiting area.
"Go get Kristen," he told the deputy.
Then he turned to me.
"Never would have thought..."
I grinned. I felt like I could fly up off the floor.
"One more thing, though," said Chief Williams and he came and put his arm around me. Charlene and the deputy were coming down the hall toward us.
He spoke very quietly next to my ear.
"You know, Billy Ray, she may not have killed her children but she still shot a man and burned him up. She's been through a lot of stuff in her life that has twisted her mind. She not right, Billy Ray. She's not right."
I took in Charlene's face as the deputy walked her up to us. She looked like an angel to me.
I whispered back to in his ear.
"She's right for me, Chief."

Then I reached out and took Charlene's hand and walked her to the glass doors.

The Chief opened a door for us and said, "Offer still stands in Jenkins, Billy Ray."

I smiled at him...my friend. "Maybe later, Chief."

****

Charlene and I walked silently in the dark up Makin Road towards home. We just made the top of the hill when I heard a yapping sound that got louder and louder as we neared the house. And there he was, New Big Dog, standing on the porch waiting for us, like he knew all along we were going to eventually show up. I looked up at the sky and I knew everything was going to be okay because each and every star was out shining down on us.

Charlene patted New Big Dog on the head and she looked at me and smiled. Then she put her arms around me and whispered in my ear, "I love you, Sweet Billy Ray, I love you."

My Charlene was back.

The End